PRAISE FOR THE REVEREND ANNABELLE DIXON COZY MYSTERY SERIES

"Absolutely wonderful!!"

"Love, love this series."

"Wonderfully descriptive settings, delightful characters, and superb storyline make this a suspenseful cozy mystery that will grab and hold your attention."

"I read it that night, and it was GREAT!"

"I couldn't put it down!"

"4 thumbs up!!!"

"It kept me up until 3am. I love it."

"As a former village Annabelle this ticks the box for me."

"Absolutely wonderful!!"

"This series keeps getting better and better."

"Annabelle, with her great intuition, caring personality, yet imperfect judgment, is a wonderful main character."

"It's fun to grab a cup of tea and pretend I'm sitting in the vicarage discussing the latest mysteries with Annabelle while she polishes off the last of the cupcakes."

"Great book - love Reverend Annabelle Dixon and can't wait to read more of her books."

"Annabelle reminds me of Agatha Christie's Miss Marple."

MURDER AT THE MANSION

ALSO BY ALISON GOLDEN

Death at the Café

Murder at the Mansion

Body in the Woods

Grave in the Garage

Horror in the Highlands

Killer at the Cult

Fireworks in France

COLLECTIONS

Books 1-4

Death at the Café

Murder at the Mansion

Body in the Woods

Grave in the Garage

Books 5-7

Horror in the Highlands

Killer at the Cult

Fireworks in France

MURDER AT THE MANSION

ALISON GOLDEN

JAMIE VOUGEOT

Cover Illustration: Rosalie Yachi Clarita

Published by Mesa Verde Publishing
P.O. Box 1002
San Carlos, CA 94070

Edited by
Marjorie Kramer

"The greatest gift is a passion for reading."
Elizabeth Hardwick

For a limited time, you can get the first books in each of my series - *Chaos in Cambridge, The Case of the Screaming Beauty, Hunted, and Mardi Gras Madness* - plus updates about new releases, promotions, and other Insider exclusives, by signing up for my mailing list at:

https://www.alisongolden.com/annabelle

CHAPTER ONE

T HE ONLY THING Annabelle didn't like about driving her royal blue Mini Cooper was that she couldn't see how pretty it looked against the lush English countryside as she did so. In her mind, the various green hues of the fields, trees, and hedgerows provided the perfect backdrop for her petite blue bullet of a car as it raced around the country lanes. She would always picture herself zooming along like an actor in a lavishly produced British television drama with an audience of millions. Happy ending guaranteed.

Annabelle loved driving. She loved driving almost as much as she loved cake, and that was saying something. Annabelle's enthusiasm for sugary treats was as well-known in the village of Upton St. Mary where she now lived as was her easy-going yet steadfast character. Going for a spin in her Mini with its go-faster stripes followed by a cup of tea and a slice of cake was her idea of a perfect summer's afternoon.

She whipped the terrier-like motor through the gentle inclines of the Cornish countryside and found it impossible not to smile. Upton St. Mary was very much the kind of village where people often smiled for no apparent reason. She was coming up to her third year as vicar of the small but dedicated community, yet the elegantly built stone walls, the unfurling landscape of green hills, and stout trees that surrounded it still took her breath away.

Though she had grown up with the hustle and bustle of working-class London, daughter of a street-savvy cabbie and a friendly, diligent cleaning lady, she had always dreamed of finding some grand version of idyllic peace. A place filled with beauty, calm, and goodness. Annabelle's soul had found it in the glow of the Lord, and her body found it in this quaint little village tucked into a beautiful corner at the very end of England. Even the frequent rains and chilly winters couldn't spoil this very British Garden of Eden for her.

The villagers, many of whom had spent their entire lives there, were just as appreciative of Upton St. Mary as their entranced reverend. Many of their pastimes and traditions involved enjoying the good-naturedness of their neighbors and their delightfully well-maintained cottages. Residents also loved nothing more than an open-air crafts fair or some other competition in which the patient, studious members of the community could display their talents in gardening, knitting, pottery, and—frequently to Annabelle's delight—baking. Retaining the village's rustic charm attracted much attention and a lot of energy attended every local issue. Whether it was a problematic pothole or a controversial building extension, the proud villagers had very strong opinions and voiced them at every opportunity.

The strictly-held conventions of the village, coupled with the speed at which gossip traveled through the close-knit community, meant that Annabelle's introduction as vicar had been greeted with reticence by some and concern by others. "A female vicar? In Upton St. Mary? What on earth will we do?" said one particularly anxious voice. "It's a slippery slope. Today a female Annabelle, tomorrow there'll be a coffee bar where the tea shop used to be!" said another.

But Annabelle was not the type to be fazed. Her dedication to church matters was unparalleled. Using her plentiful positive energy, she delivered sermons with devotion and strokes of well-appointed humor while galvanizing more than a few reluctant churchgoers to attend services more often than ever before. She was never too busy to lend a hand here or an ear there. She didn't hesitate to put on her wellies and get stuck in with the farmers. She would stop and chat with the ladies in the tea shop, navigating discussions with decorum and grace. She quickly became the presence villagers wanted at their bedside when ill and their first port of call when a dispute needed resolving fairly and with tact. In sum, Annabelle was irresistible.

Her predecessor had been male, a distinctly hairy male, and relations had been all quite straightforward. However, Annabelle's appointment had put the villagers in a quandary. How should they refer to the female vicar? Was her gender to be a cause for impropriety and social faux-pas? "Father" had long been the customary term, and now that was out of the question. Much discussion ensued on the subject until Annabelle put an end to it with her typical decisiveness and tact. The villagers were to call her "Vicar," "Reverend," or just plain "Annabelle." With their concerns addressed, everyone went on their merry way.

Yes, Annabelle had become a widely accepted and to some, a much-loved boon to the village. The fact that her dog collar was wrapped around a distinctly feminine and surprisingly elegant neck had now been forgotten (or at least ignored) by those who were perhaps a little slower to embrace the new ways of the world. She had settled into the gentle, quiet pace of life a village church position afforded with good humor and grace—making it easy for the villagers to accept her.

Annabelle eased her Mini onto the tightly woven, cobblestone streets that were at the village's center and gave a jolly wave to Mr. Hawthorne as he passed by on his daily morning bike ride. He was a mischievous gentleman of sixty who told tall tales of his youth in the local pub. While he claimed to ride his bike every morning "for the constitutional benefits," it was an open secret in the village that he rode to a secluded spot in which he could enjoy the pleasure of his pipe away from the prying eyes of his disapproving wife.

Annabelle reached a small house on the outskirts of the village, as cute and prim as she knew its' inhabitant to be. She stopped the car and got out. The sun was just beginning to sprinkle a dappled yellow light on the village. Annabelle took a deep breath of crisp, fresh air. She detected a faint whiff of something sweet and warm. She briskly locked the car door, marched to the front of the house, and knocked cheerily.

After a few moments, the door opened the tiniest of slivers revealing a pair of deep blue eyes and not much else.

"Good morning, Annabelle," said the elderly woman behind the door before she opened it wider and quickly hurried further back into the house.

"Good morning, Philippa," said Annabelle, wiping her feet on the doormat and following her through the cottage. "Why do you insist on opening the door in that manner? I feel like a door-to-door salesman. I'm sure you're not expecting anyone else."

"Better safe than sorry," said Philippa, leading the way past a paper-strewn desk into the kitchen.

"Oh, these look scrumptious!" squealed Annabelle, catching sight of the range of cakes Philippa had laid out on the kitchen table.

Philippa smiled, took the teapot, and began pouring tea.

"I'm trying something new this year. I might experiment with nuts a little. Walnuts, almonds, that sort of thing. I thought it might give me a better chance of standing out at the fair."

"Mmm," mumbled Annabelle, already chomping on a particularly rich and utterly delicious cupcake, her ravenous appetite winning the battle over ladylike reserve. "Your baking always stands out, Philippa."

"Thank you, Annabelle," Philippa chuckled, "but there's some stiff competition in Upton St. Mary. I even considered baklava at one point."

"Baklava? I haven't the foggiest idea what that might be."

"It reminds me of my youth and a trip I took to Greece. You'd love it. It's a sweet pastry drenched in honey, with nuts. *Very* continental." Philippa winked.

"Well, I say jolly well go for it!" Annabelle exclaimed, putting down the cake reluctantly and sipping at her tea.

"Oh, I couldn't, Annabelle."

"Why ever not?"

"Think of the outrage! A foreign pastry? At an English summer fête?"

Annabelle considered the point for a moment before nodding. Upton St. Mary was welcoming to new people but not nearly as benevolent to new ideas.

CHAPTER TWO

"I SEE YOU have company," Annabelle said, gesturing toward the corner of the room. Biscuit, the church's ginger tabby cat was sitting demurely by the door, lazily gazing at the two women while licking her lustrous fur.

"She dropped by last night and stayed here while I prepared the attendance and donation reports for the church. That cat visits more places around this village than you do, Annabelle."

Annabelle chuckled and reached down to urge the cat toward her. "Here, Biscuit! Here, girl!" Biscuit continued to gaze at her nonchalantly. Spurned by the feline and feeling a little foolish, Annabelle turned to Philippa and asked: "Did you feed her?"

"Nuh-uh. That cat is a complete mystery. I put some food out last night and I don't believe she took more than a mouthful."

"Hmm."

"The strange thing is that she's putting on the pounds."

"Well, I suspect half the village is probably feeding her," said Annabelle, picking up her cupcake again. "Lucky girl!"

"Indeed. Well, cats are fortunate in that they don't need to worry about such things," Philippa said. "Unlike the rest of us." Philippa brought her teacup to her face for an uncommonly long time. Philippa was a tiny twig of a woman.

"Philippa!" Annabelle said.

"Now, Reverend, I only say this out of concern. None of us are getting any younger. It would be a shame if you struggled to find a young man because of that sweet tooth of yours."

Annabelle tried to protest but her mouth was full of soft spongy cupcake. She put the cupcake down indignantly and furrowed her brow.

"And if the rumors about Inspector Nicholls are true..." Philippa continued.

"Philippa!" Annabelle said again sternly. Philippa raised her hands in apology.

For a few moments, the two women sat in a silence that grew tenser by the second, occasionally pierced by the clink of teacup on china, their eyes fixed upon the large window that looked out onto the deep woods behind Philippa's cottage.

"What rumors?" said Annabelle eventually, unable to hold in her curiosity any longer.

"Well," Philippa said with a twinkle in her eye. She leaned forward, her elbows on the table, her teacup light in her hands. She needed no further invitation to indulge in her primary passion—gossip. "I've got some news."

Annabelle tapped her teaspoon against her cup. Philippa ignored her and continued. "As you know,

Dorothy's sister-in-law has a son who works in Truro in a baker's shop just a couple of streets away from the police station. He was the one who told us that the inspector was married. Dorothy's sister-in-law can be a bit unreliable, but this was confirmed by Mr. Higginbotham whose daughter lives down the road from the newsagent where the inspector gets his paper..."

"Philippa, please. If it will take us the entire morning, I'd rather move on to another topic."

"Sorry, Reverend. Well, essentially, Inspector Nicholls is single again. Now might be your chance. Oh, you would make a lovely couple. He's such a dashing young man. Terribly smart. Annabelle and a police inspector. It would be like something from a novel!"

Annabelle sighed. "I appreciate your concern, Philippa, but I'm in no rush to begin courting, thank you."

"Whatever you wish," Philippa said, barely concealing a wry smirk. She paused. "Though you may soon find yourself with competition if you're not careful."

Annabelle furrowed her brow again. She hated the gossip and rumor-mongering that passed for conversation with Philippa, yet the wily church secretary had a talent for piquing her interest. "How so?"

"Well, a handsome young man like that. He's soon to be snapped up!"

"Let's change the subject, Philippa. What else is going on?"

"That new person has moved into the large country house outside the village on the Arden Road."

"Ah, yes. I did hear something about that."

"Well, he's here, and he's already causing quite the stir."

"Really?"

"Why, yes. I hear he's been inviting all kinds of women to the house since he moved in. There's been loud music, the sounds of laughter. Parties. Can you *imagine*? It's extremely concerning. Those sorts are ten a penny in London," Philippa said, growing visibly irate, "but we don't want them *here*. This is the last place to find... that kind of person. People say he doesn't even have a denomination!"

"Calm down, Philippa. I'm sure he's a perfectly nice man. This is all conjecture. People running wild with their imaginations."

"I hope so, Annabelle. I really do."

"What is he doing here?"

"That's just it. Nobody knows. What if he's running some sort of... well... a devilish establishment!"

"Why would you think he was doing that? Philippa, please. I wish you wouldn't allow yourself such ridiculous flights of fancy. He's probably just had a housewarming party. Or had friends up for the weekend."

"But Reverend, to invite not one, but multiple women to..."

"Look, I'll pay him a visit today. We need to welcome our new neighbor. Let me speak with him and set everyone's fears to rest."

"That sounds like a good idea, Annabelle. Perhaps you're right."

"Do you happen to know his name?"

Philippa pretended to ponder a moment before saying, "I believe it's John Cartwright. Yes, yes, that's it."

"Very well. I shall speak to Mr. John Cartwright myself. Extend the hand of neighborly friendship, as it were. In the meantime, I do hope you can refrain from indulging in these fantastical stories, Philippa. They don't help anyone."

"Oh, I will, Annabelle," said Philippa. Annabelle knew

she meant it, but she also knew that Philippa had a deep and fertile imagination the contents of which she couldn't help sharing as fact. She had to accept it. Be it Philippa's penchant for gossip or ignoring glorious cakes, some things were beyond her control.

CHAPTER THREE

ANNABELLE LEFT PHILIPPA'S house with a sense of foreboding. Nothing good ever came from gossip. The rumors that occasionally spread rapidly around the village tended toward the outrageous with little basis in reality and were often in stark contrast to Upton St. Mary's idyllic scenery. Annabelle couldn't shake a heavy feeling that tainted the clear, pure atmosphere of the morning.

What *was* going on at the big house on Arden Road? Was it just high jinks? Or was there something more sinister going on, as Philippa imagined? It seemed unlikely but Annabelle had to concede that even a stopped clock is right twice a day.

After revving the engine of her blue Mini and waving cheerily at Philippa, Annabelle turned the car around and carefully trundled on toward the church, mindful of both the early hour and the speed limit.

Pushing her troubled thoughts away, Annabelle paid a quick pastoral visit to the Wilshere family who had just returned from the hospital with their new baby and who would no doubt have been awake for hours. The Wilsheres were a jolly kind, the sort of people who had worked the land and served the good folk of the village for generations. The parents, Mitchell and Michelle, were both rotund and bubbly and with their puffy cheeks that were prone to flush, they were much like babies themselves.

Being that this was their firstborn, the parents were still doting nervously over the new baby boy when Annabelle arrived. She cooed and cuddled the infant and the Wilsheres exchanged looks of pride when he smiled at Annabelle as she held him. Annabelle politely declined their appeals to sit and have tea but left the home feeling more serene and content thanks to their warmth and good humor.

She absent-mindedly continued toward the church enjoying the hypnotic greens and browns that passed by her and the plain stone cottages that provided a contrasting backdrop to brightly blooming hanging baskets that overflowed with pink, purple, white, and blue flowers. As she did so, she thought of the inspector. Single again? Maybe she should pay him a brief visit, just to see how he was getting on. It had been a while since they last spoke, and he *had* looked rather handsome when she last saw him....

Annabelle buried the thought by remembering John Cartwright. She really should meet this newcomer and nip all the rumor-mongering in the bud. If she didn't, she knew that in no time he would be considered a monster and possibly confronted with pitchforks at dawn. She chuckled to herself at the thought and on a whim took a turn away from the direction of the church and up the long and winding Arden Road out of the village.

Annabelle had not had reason to visit the estate before. There were, in fact, a few such large properties at short distances from the village, though not much was known about the owners. Most of them appeared in the village just frequently enough to keep rumors at bay. They were older sorts often from distinguished families, left to enjoy the serenity of their large piles as their offspring ventured into the metropolitan cities of the world to seek their fortunes (or squander it, as some suggested.) Others were irregular visitors to the area, driving down from London for the occasional weekend "in the country." The villagers viewed neither type with particular fondness.

Mystery had always shrouded the property to which Annabelle was now traveling. Locals referred to it as *Woodlands Manor*. It was tucked deep inside a thick wood. While many sought large properties for their magnificent views and peacefulness that such a mellow and sleepy part of the world provided, this secretive and secluded estate had garnered little attention. Until now.

Annabelle turned her car off the smooth surface of Arden Road and onto the grassy, overgrown path that led blindly into the trees. The wheels of the Mini jostled over the ground giving Annabelle a good shaking until she emerged yards further on to an expanse that made her squeal. "Crikey!"

The grounds of *Woodlands Manor* were immaculate. Vivid green lawns extended away in front of Annabelle, pressing up against the wild woods like some vast oasis in the desert. Delicately pruned hedges and tastefully arranged patches of irises, roses, and petunias threw elegant splashes of color onto the gardens like an impressionist painting. A gently curving gravel path extended deep between the guiding hedgerows, leading the way to the Elizabethan mansion that stood large and proud as though surveying the beauty of its surroundings.

Annabelle eased her car forward slowly, taking in the

impressive scene. Had these lavish grounds always been here? A secret tucked away out of sight. She rounded a large fountain that stood tall on the open area facing the property, parking the car in front of the stone steps that led to its gigantic oak doors. As she got out of the car, Annabelle allowed herself one more look at the sight of the lovely mansion grounds before spinning on her heels and marching in her characteristically determined manner up the steps. After a couple of enthusiastic whacks of the heavy iron knocker, a young, attractive woman in jeans and a t-shirt opened the door. She had golden blond hair that framed her pretty face, and full, rounded lips.

"Hello?" she said curiously, before noticing Annabelle's clerical collar. Her soft musical voice was upbeat. "Oh. How may I help you?"

"Good morning," Annabelle said in her most cheerful voice, "I'm Reverend Annabelle Dixon. I'm vicar of St. Mary's church in the village. I recently learned that someone had moved into this magnificent property, so I wished to extend a welcome."

"I see. That's very kind of you, Reverend," the young woman said, politely. "I'm afraid Sir John cannot meet you at the moment, however."

"Oh?"

"Yes. He has just begun his daily meditation. After that, ablutions, then a simple breakfast."

"Really?" Annabelle said, considering this information. "Well, reflection is very important and time is difficult to find these days. Do you happen to know when he will be available?"

"He's not to be disturbed for another hour yet. If you can return then, I'm sure he'd love to chat with you."

"Wonderful," Annabelle said, clapping her hands

together, "I shall call upon you in an hour. Thank you very much."

"You're welcome, Reverend. I'm sure Sir John will appreciate your visit."

"I look forward to speaking with him. See you shortly!"

The woman nodded and closed the door as Annabelle jogged down the steps and settled into her Mini. As she urged the car around the fountain and back along the satisfyingly crunchy gravel toward Arden Road, Annabelle thought about what the woman had said. *Sir* John Cartwright? Philippa had mentioned nothing regarding a man with a knighthood. Could this elusive stranger really be a knight of the realm?

Despite herself, Annabelle felt some skepticism. Such people had reputations that preceded them. Sir John Cartwright had arrived with little fanfare or foreknowledge. Was it possible that the title wasn't real? It wouldn't be the first time a person of wealth had faked a title to gain social standing and acceptance into moneyed circles. Members of such classes were above checking credentials, making it easy to be passed off as a person of nobility. But if he were a knight, how had the title come about? And what of the women who had allegedly visited *Woodlands Manor*? Legions of them, if Philippa was to be believed. The woman who had greeted Annabelle was rather young. She had seemed perfectly nice and respectable, yet Annabelle had detected a note of reserve. The young woman had not even offered her name....

Annabelle shook herself. She was getting as bad as Philippa. She would return later to find out the truth. Until then, there was much to be done in the parish.

CHAPTER FOUR

"STOP IT, ANNABELLE. You'll be grabbing a pitchfork of your own soon." Annabelle was still chiding herself for speculating about the new owner of *Woodlands Manor* when she stopped outside the bakery to buy some bread. She was hosting lunch later for the ladies of the Women's Institute who were meeting to discuss their idea for a fundraising event that involved a bawdy revue and bingo night. Annabelle had reservations about the wisdom of such a plan and thought some plain egg and cress sandwiches might be mundane enough to lower the temperatures of some of the more irrepressible members of the club. She staggered out of the bakery wrestling three baguettes and a dozen rolls.

When she got outside, the sunlight was blinding. Her breath left her for a moment as a young man she didn't recognize bumped into her. "Oh!" The baguettes scraped her forehead and her bag split. Rolls fell everywhere.

"Sorry!" the young man said. "Let me help you." Together they retrieved the rolls, dusting them off as

Annabelle got herself another bag. "Five-second rule, right?"

"I guess," Annabelle replied. "I won't tell if you won't." Annabelle seriously doubted she could bring herself to use the rolls now but it seemed churlish to say so. "Thank you for helping me."

"No problem, have a nice day," the man said. He walked away quickly and turned a corner.

When she got to St. Mary's, Annabelle parked her car and went inside. She busied herself with church duties until the phone rang.

"Reverend?"

"Yes, Philippa?"

"I've completed the reports."

"Wonderful! Thank you."

"Of course." There was a pause.

"Was there anything else, Philippa?"

There was another pause before Philippa spoke again. "Well, I feel terribly awkward bringing it up..."

"What's the problem?"

"It's just that I like to know my portion sizes. Waste is a terrible sin, after all."

"I'm not sure I follow, Philippa."

"Well..."

Annabelle waited a few moments before urging the church secretary on again. "Do tell me, Philippa. You'll have me awfully worried if not."

"Well, it's the cupcakes."

"The cupcakes?"

"Yes."

"What about them?"

"The walnut cupcakes. The ones I laid out this morning."

"Yes, I know."

"How many did you eat? Oh, this is embarrassing."

Annabelle struggled with her memory for a second, then said: "I believe I had two. Yes. That's it. I certainly had two."

"No more than that?"

"No. Definitely just two. Why?"

"You're sure you didn't have three? Do forgive me for asking."

"I recall our chat perfectly, Philippa. I had two cupcakes—one with each cup of tea."

"I see," Philippa said, trailing off on a note of disappointment.

Annabelle sighed and quickly checked her watch. "Was there anything else, Philippa?"

"No, no. That's all, Annabelle," Philippa said, her dismay apparent.

"Very well. I'll speak to you later today then. Thank you very much for the reports."

"Of course. Thank *you* very much. Goodbye."

What was all *that* about? Annabelle pondered the call as she rang off before remembering her appointment at *Woodlands Manor*. She looked at her watch and rushed out of the church, back into her car. It was turning out to be a rather eventful day, and it had barely begun.

Once again, Annabelle headed out to the discreet track that led through the trees to the lavish grounds of *Woodlands Manor*. Just over an hour had passed since her last visit, and her curiosity had only grown in that time. She found herself chomping at the bit to see this mysterious newcomer for herself; this meditating nobleman, the source of so much conjecture in Upton St. Mary.

Annabelle spun the Mini around the fountain, bringing

it to a stop with a confident press of the brakes. She climbed out and marched up the steps to the intimidating doors. They were so tall that even Annabelle, with her five-foot eleven-inch frame, felt tiny in their presence. She thumped the knocker again and stepped back.

The youthful face of the blond woman appeared as she opened the door. She smiled as she recognized Annabelle. "Hel—"

A wild, bloodcurdling scream echoed down through the mansion from somewhere above. It was loud, powerful, and frightening. The smiles of both women froze and then vanished, their expressions turning to horror as their eyes locked, and they found themselves stunned, shaken, and shocked by the beastly sound.

CHAPTER FIVE

ANNABELLE SPRANG INTO action as the young woman's hand flew to her mouth in horror. The woman stared at Annabelle with eyes that were wide with fear. Paying her no mind, Annabelle pushed past her. She ran into the house and scanned the huge entrance hall looking for anything suspicious, before taking the stairs two at a time to the landing on the second floor.

In emergencies, Annabelle's clumsy charm and humble self-deprecation would give way to a keen wit and sharp reflexes, and within seconds of reaching the next floor a door at the end of the passage caught her attention. The door handle was more elegant than those of other doors and framed by two perfectly preserved Ming vases on intricately carved pedestals. This must be the master bedroom—the source of that terrifying scream. She rushed toward it. The blond woman caught up with her and scampered close behind as if Annabelle were a shield that would protect her from whatever lurked behind the door.

"Fiddlesticks!" Annabelle said as she grabbed the handle. The door was locked.

"I'll get the keys from the cloakroom," the blond woman said, her voice still musical despite the fear that made it shake.

Annabelle nodded, and the woman ran down the landing back to the stairs. She spun so quickly onto the first step that a last-minute grab of the banister was the only thing that stopped her from tumbling down them. Loathe to wait for keys, however, Annabelle grabbed the door handle once more and leaned into it, expecting nothing but resistance. Much to her surprise, the door moved. It was only slight at first, but then the old handle's weak mechanism gave way and the door swung wide open under the force of Annabelle's weight. She burst into the room.

The scene that confronted Annabelle was nothing short of astonishing. The room, much as she had expected, was large and elegant. A wide, antique bed sat against the far wall, and to one side there was an oak desk. On the other side, three large windows reached up toward the high ceiling and down to within a foot of the floor allowing pale morning light to fill the room.

The middle window was wide open, and beneath it lay the spread-eagled body of a man Annabelle assumed to be John Cartwright. Embedded deep in the middle of his chest was a single arrow. It cleanly pierced his loose shirt and protruded from his heart like a macabre signpost.

Annabelle rushed toward the prone figure. She quickly placed her fingers on the man's neck and waited, but Annabelle knew she wouldn't feel a pulse. In her time as vicar, she had seen the passing of many, almost as many as had been born, and she had developed an instinct about such things. She had known the moment she opened the door that Sir John Cartwright was no more.

She knelt solemnly beside the man's body, crossed herself, and clasped her hands in a quickly mumbled, sincere prayer. Once she was done, she opened her eyes and stood, listening to the silence that always seemed to follow the end of human life. As a servant of the Lord, Annabelle was accustomed to death, but she had seen nothing as shocking as this. This was almost certainly murder, death of a vastly different type to the natural and godly kind that Upton St. Mary was commonly home to.

Cautious of wasting time, Annabelle fumbled for a number in her cell phone. She called the local police station.

"Vicar! Been a while since I heard from you!" said a chirpy voice on the other end of the phone.

"I noticed. We haven't seen you in church for a while, Constable Raven."

"Um, well, yes. Busy, you know..."

"Never mind. Something serious has occurred. I need you to come as quickly as possible. I'm at *Woodlands Manor*, the estate on Arden Road. Do you know it?"

"Yes, I know it. That doesn't sound too good," PC Raven said. "I'll be on my way as soon as..."

"Now, Constable," Annabelle said firmly. She could almost hear the look of surprise her brusqueness caused the constable. She pictured his eyebrows rising to his hairline.

"What is it, Reverend?"

"Murder, Constable. A man is dead." There was another pause. Annabelle heard a mug slamming against a desktop.

"I'm on my way."

When the call ended, Annabelle looked around the

room again. She gazed out of the open window at the dense woods that wove themselves into the hills at the back of the mansion and remembered the young woman's earlier promise to fetch the keys to the master bedroom. Where had she got to? Surely she would have found the keys by now. With a deepening sense that something curious was afoot, Annabelle set out to look for her.

Minutes later, Annabelle was confident she had searched every spot in the grand house. There was no sign of the woman. As she looked, Annabelle hoped that her disappearance was down to fear getting the better of her. Perhaps she had come back and glimpsed the body as Annabelle prayed. Perhaps she was somewhere in the house, cowering in fear. Annabelle liked to think the best of people—until proved otherwise. However, after searching all the major rooms, Annabelle had to resign herself to the truth. The young woman was gone.

CHAPTER SIX

CONSTABLE JIM RAVEN was well into his thirties, but the constant glint in his brown eyes, as well as his boyish, cheeky grin, made him appear much younger. It was a well-known joke that he'd only become a police officer to avoid getting into trouble himself. He was the type to join children in a street game or take a little longer than was strictly necessary ensuring everything was in order at the local pastry shop. The truth be known, his *laissez-faire* approach to police work would have had him reprimanded almost daily were it not for the scarcity of criminal elements in Upton St. Mary. It also helped that Jim Raven was the perfect type of police officer for this quiet community.

With a wink and a joke, Jim could diffuse even the most hostile of disputes, and his breezy, infectious manner could persuade the most stubborn village local to see the funny side. Children of the village would even confess their transgressions to him like an elder brother. If there were a traffic accident or pub fight, Jim could be relied upon to resolve the situation in an amicable exchange of verbal agreements, handshakes, and gentle scoldings. However, he had never had to deal with murder before.

After Annabelle's phone call, Raven jumped into a police car and sped away from the station, forgetting even to put his siren on until he had completed half the journey. To Jim, sirens had proven more useful when giving villagers a funny fright or for children to play with as he gave them a lift home than for actual police work.

He reached the fountain in front of *Woodlands Manor* and screeched to a stop. The tires of his small police car slid across the gravel, giving the constable a guilty sense of drama and excitement. He turned off the sirens, and leaving the flashing blue light on, got out of the car and fixed his hat firmly onto his head.

Jim entered the open entrance of the house to find Annabelle sitting on an upholstered bench beside the staircase. She was staring at the floor and frowning. The two knew each other very well, having frequently crossed paths amid the affairs of the village. Their shared love of laughter had instigated many a romantic rumor. But Annabelle towered over the police officer by a full half foot which made them an odd couple when standing near to one another, not least when Annabelle wore heels. Eventually, the contrast between Annabelle's diligent and sharp mind and Jim's perpetual merry mischief making forced even the most persistent of matchmakers to give up.

As he saw Annabelle sitting there, Jim braced himself for a long story. He knew Annabelle well enough to be aware of how she could regale events in fulsome detail with elaborate and expressive language, many digressions, only coming to an end when she was fully spent. This time, however, Annabelle simply stood silently and led the way up the staircase. Jim followed behind, growing increasingly nervous at the absence of talk.

When Annabelle reached the master bedroom with the constable close behind, she stepped aside to reveal the still figure of Sir John Cartwright. Immediately, Jim turned around and put his hand over his mouth. He leaped toward the private bathroom. After examining the inside of the toilet bowl more closely than he would have liked and splashing water onto his face, he returned to the bedroom. Annabelle stood where he'd left her, in the doorway, surveying the scene as if looking for something she'd forgotten.

"I'm sorry, Reverend. This is the first time I've seen a dead body."

"It's alright, Jim."

"It just caught me by surprise, is all."

"Of course."

"And I've had this stomach bug for days. I shouldn't have had that fry-up this morn..."

Annabelle turned to him. "Don't worry, Jim. I won't tell anyone unless it's absolutely necessary."

Jim smiled. "Thank you. Much appreciated." He turned slowly to look at the body again, pressing his lips and tightening his stomach this time. "Is this how you found him?"

"Yes," replied Annabelle, still deep in thought.

"We should be careful to preserve the crime scene."

"Absolutely. I do hope that there weren't any clues in the bathroom."

Constable Raven's smooth-shaven cheeks went red with embarrassment. "I don't think so," he said nervously.

"Hmm, me neither," muttered Annabelle.

"I'll go radio for Inspector Nicholls," said Jim. "He'll need to come from the city." He pulled his radio from his lapel and returned to the passage.

Left on her own in the bedroom, it was Annabelle who found herself blushing now.

CHAPTER SEVEN

I NSPECTOR MIKE NICHOLLS strode into the
bedroom along with two other officers from Truro
police station. As the inspector walked confidently
across the room, Annabelle forgot what she was saying to
Constable Raven. She noticed how Nicholls scanned the
room with sharp, piercing eyes, his broad, powerful shoulders shifting casually beneath his trench coat as if murder
were an everyday occurrence for him. She wondered if he
had chosen the cut of his suit to accentuate his commanding
height. She gazed at the short stubble that failed to conceal
his strong bone structure and couldn't help imagining what
it might feel like under her hand.

"Good to see you, Constable," the inspector said,
shaking Raven's hand vigorously, "and you, Reverend."

Annabelle applied all the strength she could muster to
keep her knees from failing her. "Oh, yes," was all she could
manage.

"The pathologist should be here any minute now. Mind
telling me what happened?"

"Well, Reverend Dixon here called me about a..." Raven began.

"I heard a man had moved into the village," interrupted Annabelle, raising her hand to silence the policeman and sidling over to place herself at the center of the inspector's attention. "A Sir John Cartwright. There was some gossip about him among the villagers."

"What kind of gossip?" asked the inspector.

"Oh, nothing out of the ordinary. The typical kind of unsubstantiated rumor that sometimes blows up in a small community. You'd be surprised at how fertile some imaginations can be when seeds are planted." Annabelle was aware she was over-egging things but couldn't help herself.

"I understand. Please continue, Reverend."

"Well, I decided to pay the gentleman a visit so that I could welcome him to our community. You know, it's dreadfully important to get to know the people you live alongside, Inspector. I make it a habit to visit newcomers. And so about two hours ago, I dropped by, and was greeted at the door by a young woman."

"Where is she?" said the inspector, looking around the room.

"She left. I can't find her."

"Can you describe her?"

"Blond hair, to the nape of her neck. Blue eyes. Early twenties, I should say. Attractive."

"No name?"

"No. Earlier this morning she told me Sir John was busy meditating and would not be available for an hour. I left and returned just over sixty minutes later. The young woman opened the door again, and right then there was the most chilling scream from inside this house."

"The dead man?"

"I believe so. I ran inside to discover the source of this horrendous sound. I am not one to shirk during times of danger or crisis, Inspector." Annabelle looked into the inspector's eyes, as if trying to communicate telepathically the subtext of her speech. *I am a very brave person.* "Eventually I came up to the bedroom," she continued. "The door seemed locked at first, and the woman said she would find the key. She left, but I managed to open the door, only to discover *this...*" Annabelle gestured toward the dead body, "truly horrifying scene."

The inspector exchanged a glance with Raven who had been edged over ever so slightly during Annabelle's recital of events. "It's always a shock to see a body," he said.

"That's very perceptive of you, Inspector," Annabelle replied.

"Especially when it's a case of murder, as this appears to be," Nicholls added.

"It must take such strength to face this kind of horrible brutality day in, day out. It takes a man with real fortitude and conviction to do so in the name of justice," Annabelle breathed.

"I suppose. It's my job, really, Reverend."

"So stoic, so noble, so..."

A woman with the blackest hair Annabelle had ever seen entered the bedroom. "Ah, Harper!" exclaimed the inspector.

Harper Jones was one of the finest pathologists in the north of England before she moved south to the sunnier climes of Cornwall to marry the owner of a local bicycle shop. A strict believer in leading by example, her extensive fitness regime and dedicated diet had given her an appearance that belied her forty-seven years. She still warranted stolen glances from men half her age. Her silky black hair cascaded around her face and a pair of hazel eyes probed and investigated everything in their path.

"Inspector," she said, nodding a perfunctory greeting to the assembled group. She didn't hesitate as she made her way over to the victim's body. "Reverend. Jim."

Without ceremony, Harper dropped her doctor's bag beside the corpse and knelt. The inspector stepped toward the open window, Annabelle shuffling closely behind. As the pathologist began probing the body, rooting in her bag for various instruments, the inspector flipped open his notebook and began scribbling.

"Reverend..."

"Yes?" said Annabelle, rather more hastily than was necessary.

"How long has it been since you heard the scream?"

Annabelle checked her watch. "Just over an hour. I found the body, prayed for a minute or two, then I took a short while to look for the woman. Constable Raven arrived about ten minutes later, and a few minutes after that he called you. All in all, I suppose just over twenty minutes passed between our discovery and the call to you. You arrived around forty minutes later, making an hour."

"I see," Nicholls said. Annabelle watched him as he stood in front of the window, holding his pen to simulate the arrow's trajectory. She noticed a police officer scanning the grounds at the edge of the woods outside. She looked back at the inspector, his brow lined with frustration.

"Is something wrong, Inspector?"

"Hmm, I can't figure out why he's lying where he is."

"Oh?"

"He is facing the window. How would someone have shot him from such close range?"

Annabelle looked from the body to the open sash window and back to the inspector's confused expression. "Might I offer an idea?"

CHAPTER EIGHT

THE INSPECTOR LOOKED up from his notebook. "Of course, Reverend."

"I mean, it's probably nonsense," Annabelle chuckled. "I'm sure it's just a silly idea, and I'm wasting your time. I probably shouldn't even be bothering you right now."

"No, no. Go ahead."

"Well, he was meditating, so he was probably sitting cross-legged just in front of the window. Look, his legs are crossed at the ankle. If he had been standing—and this is just a wild assumption, please ignore me if I'm being terribly ignorant—I would imagine his legs splayed out more."

"Hmm," the inspector mumbled, tapping his pen against his lips.

Annabelle continued, spurred by the excitement of having Inspector Nicholl's full attention. "The window reaches low to the ground so his head and upper body would have been visible from outside, even while sitting. The arrow is embedded in his chest too, in the part that could have been seen. It seems entirely plausible to me. Perhaps... maybe... I don't know... but perhaps he was shot from outside." Annabelle's confidence faltered. "Forget I said anything, it's probably ridiculous."

But the inspector listened, and after a few moments of pondering, pen-gesticulating, and note-scribbling, he looked at Annabelle with an uncharacteristically warm smile. "I think you're most likely correct, Reverend. Some keen observation skills you have there."

Annabelle felt all the blood rush out of her legs and into her cheeks. There were times she wished she could loosen her dog collar, and this was certainly one of them. She wrestled with her suddenly parched throat, before squeaking out a high-pitched "yes" and deciding against uttering anything more ambitious. The inspector went back to his notebook, leaving Annabelle to gaze at his strongly defined jaw.

"Looks like he died well over an hour ago. Much before you heard that scream," Harper Jones announced suddenly.

"That doesn't make any sense," Inspector Nicholls said.

"No, it doesn't," Annabelle agreed.

Harper shrugged the statement off. "I'll need everyone out of here. We'll take the body away and I'll confirm the time of death after the post-mortem." Harper abruptly turned and walked off, giving instructions to a medical assistant who stood by the door.

"Right, well, we're mostly done here," the inspector said. "Let's leave this room to SOCO, see if they can winkle anything more out of it, but I've seen enough for now." He followed Harper out of the room, Annabelle and PC Raven close behind.

Outside the house, several cars were parked at all manner of angles around the fountain, including an ambulance. Paramedics, Truro police, and scenes of crimes officers paced back and forth. In the melee, Annabelle lost sight of the inspector. She frantically searched for him as the ambulance left and officers got in their cars.

"Inspector! Inspector!" she called wildly. She spotted him about to get into his unmarked police car. She half-ran, half-walked across the gravel drive as daintily as she could, which wasn't very daintily at all. She had to move so quickly that she was panting when she reached him.

"Yes, Reverend?"

"Is there... anything... I can do... to help?" Annabelle gasped.

"I doubt it, Reverend. There's not much to go on and a lot to find out. I get the impression we've only seen a small portion of whatever's happened here."

"Really?"

"An arrow shot from outside the building makes it tricky. No bullet to match, no gunpowder sprays, no fingerprints. No sound, even. We've got no witnesses. I've had my men search the house top to bottom, as well as the grounds, just in case our culprit or that woman was hiding somewhere. Nothing. On top of all that, the scream happened *after* the man was dead. That's going to make me rack my brain for days unless we get a quick answer. We're a long way from solving this one, but leave it to us. My team will get to work."

"Yes, the villagers will be most concerned, but I shall tell them the case is in your safe hands. Could the scream really have happened after the murder?" Annabelle said.

"If Dr. Jones says so, then it's the case. She's as reliable as a rock, Harper is. As much as I wish she weren't, sometimes."

"What will you do now, Inspector?"

"Well, we need a suspect. And you're the only one I can

think of right now."

Annabelle found herself lost for words. Inspector Nicholl's face was deadpan.

"Ha! Relax, Reverend," the inspector chuckled. "Just a joke. You're far too saintly for any of this nasty business."

"Oh," breathed Annabelle, seconds away from blacking out entirely. "Good one."

"Actually, there may be something you could do for me after all."

"Whatever it is, Inspector, just say the word."

"Well, you mentioned some rumors that were flying around regarding the dead man."

"Yes."

"There's probably nothing to them, as you said, but just to be on the safe side, I'd like to know what people were thinking. We'll see what we can find out about the victim's past, but sometimes even an unsubstantiated rumor provides a good enough motive for some people. And often there are kernels of truth in rumors. I know a lot of people confide in you, Reverend, so perhaps you could get a feel for what people were saying about him. There might be something there."

"Of course, Inspector. That makes perfect sense."

"If you hear anything, just let me know."

"Likewise. Please contact me if you find anything, Inspector."

They exchanged smiles, and Nicholls opened the door of his car and got inside. After checking his phone and giving her a wave, he set off. As the car moved, Annabelle glimpsed herself in the wing mirror. She was sweating profusely, her hair a mess, and her cassock askew from all her running. As the inspector rounded the fountain, she gritted her teeth. "Bother!"

CHAPTER NINE

ANNABELLE MARCHED BACK toward her Mini exchanging nods with members of the SOCO team that were still going back and forth to the property. The sun was high and bright. The air remained crisp and cool. It was just calm enough to hear birds singing. It was barely noon, yet Annabelle had seen more drama that morning than was usual for an entire month. She put her Mini into gear and set off. A good drive always soothed her, but her mind had twisted into too many knots for her to relax. Questions pricked at her like troublesome thorns and the words of the inspector danced on the fringes of her thoughts; *"We've only seen a small portion of whatever's happened here."*

Murder was the last thing Annabelle expected in Upton St. Mary. Until then, the greatest scandal she had encountered in the quiet village had been the alleged theft of Mr. Maitland's prize-winning marrow. Those had been dark days indeed, with accusations flying in all directions. It had been one of the most divisive events in recent Upton St. Mary history. The question, "So who do *you* think took Mr.

Maitland's marrow?" had been whispered across many a dinner table.

In the spirit of community and after days of investigation and questioning, Annabelle finally cracked the case. She spoke to the concerned villagers after her Sunday sermon and outlined her discovery. She had sifted through a turn of events—part coincidence, part negligence, and part farce—and finally deduced that the nearly blind Mrs. Niles had mistaken the marrow for a misshapen pumpkin and taken it home from the summer fair. There, she promptly cooked it into a bland soup that was thrown away forthwith. Villagers were disappointed at this outcome but satisfied the mystery had been solved and happy it turned out to be an innocent mistake. But it was a chapter of the village's history best forgotten in Annabelle's humble opinion.

Sir John Cartwright was no missing vegetable, however, though in much the same way and for the same reason, Annabelle felt duty-bound to dig into this mystery. This was her village, her congregation. It was her responsibility to root out evil, just as it was to praise the joy and spread the love that was abundant in her chosen corner of the world.

But Annabelle struggled to make sense of the incident. As she drove along, she relived the events of the morning multiple times. She talked to herself as she drove toward the church, hoping that by speaking out loud she would find some sense to the situation. Unfortunately, she simply couldn't find any. Everything seemed to happen in the wrong order and for no reason. The scream *after* the death. The young woman who had exhibited no signs of malice, who had invited Annabelle to the house a second time but yet who disappeared immediately after the scream. Even the method of death was unusual. Annabelle had never heard of someone being killed with an arrow.

And finally, Sir John Cartwright—a man shrouded in mystery, barely known in the village. A man who had received visits from mysterious women. A man whose title drew many questions. And what had been the blond woman's relationship to him?

Annabelle reached the churchyard and spun the Mini into her regular parking spot, far more haphazardly than usual. As she got out of the car, Philippa called to her from the church steps.

"Reverend! Reverend!"

Annabelle walked toward her, straightening her cassock and palming down her hair.

"Hello, Philippa. I take it you've brought the reports?"

"Yes, Reverend, they're on your desk." Philippa's expression grew more concerned as Annabelle drew closer. "Oh, Annabelle, you look dreadful! Has something happened?"

"Thank you, Philippa. For the reports, that is, not your comment on my appearance. Yes, actually, something terrible has indeed happened."

"Let's go into the cottage. I'll make you a nice cup of tea and some sandwiches. I'm sure you haven't eaten for hours."

"That would be wonderful, Philippa."

"And you can tell me all about your morning."

St. Mary's church was the centerpiece of the small village. Its size was far larger than the congregation required and the tall, pointed spire could be seen for miles. Annabelle fantasized it reached higher than any point in Cornwall. The church's Gothic design and size were imposing. England's most turbulent weather had assailed the grey stone for centuries but had had almost no effect at all. The church was as strong and proud as the day it was built. The arched windows contained some of the most intricate and awe-inspiring stained glass in South West England while a huge bell, bigger than any man, rang a tone so rich and powerful that people could hear it in fields far beyond Upton St. Mary's borders.

Annabelle would sometimes gaze at the impervious structure and the equally impressive oak trees that framed it. She often wondered at the generations of people that had gathered there, the children raised in its vast shadow, and the important part it had played in the lives of Upton St. Mary's people. To one side of the church lay the cemetery, its gravel path weaving between the tombstones. There were benches where locals would rest and contemplate. On the other side of the church, among well-maintained borders flourishing with brightly colored flowers, many of which had grown from seeds and cuttings gifted by enthusiastic gardeners in the village, sat the white-walled cottage Annabelle called home.

It was a small house. It had red window and door frames and a thatched roof that, despite requiring plenty of expensive maintenance, Annabelle adored so much that she had squealed with delight on seeing it. She had wasted no time at all in making herself at home in the twee little cottage and had cultivated a garden that, while unable to compete with the best in Upton St. Mary, was a source of great pride.

Both within and without, the cottage had become a testament to the humor, patience, and kindliness of its owner. Cheerful, ceramic gnomes stood proudly among the bellflowers, sweet williams, and hollyhocks in the traditionally English wildflower garden. Beside it, a well-maintained cherry orchard complemented Annabelle's colorful flowers perfectly and was the site of her beehive, a buzzing community, that like that of Upton St. Mary, she attended to daily.

Inside the charming little cottage, gaudy knick-knacks and souvenirs sat atop handmade shelves and dressers. One needed only to glance at the soft, inviting sofa and mismatched armchairs with their colorful, patterned cushions to find signs of the Reverend's lively and fun personality. Her extensive book collection covered almost an entire wall of the living room and was a constant surprise to visitors who found it difficult to believe that the energetic Annabelle could sit in one place long enough to read a book. The cottage by the church was small—there wasn't much room to entertain—but it was intimate and warm, and Annabelle loved it.

After she had checked the church and said another prayer for John Cartwright, Annabelle walked over to the cottage to find Philippa. As she went through to the kitchen, Annabelle was pleased to discover a pot of hot tea and a plate of sandwiches on the table—plus another plate of cupcakes beside them.

"Sit down, Annabelle. You look like you could do with a rest."

"Thank you, Philippa. It's been a terribly eventful morning."

"Whatever happened?" asked Philippa, pouring the tea as Annabelle bit into a sandwich. Annabelle's mother had always told her sandwiches before cake, and she always listened to her mother.

"There's been a death."

Philippa's eyes widened, and she balked, causing hot tea to spill on the grained wood of the oak table.

"Oh dear, I'm sorry, Reverend." Philippa grabbed a cloth almost instantaneously and wiped away the spill. "May I ask who? Anyone I know?"

"John Cartwright. *Sir* John Cartwright."

CHAPTER TEN

P HILIPPA'S EYES WIDENED even further, and
her mouth dropped open with surprise. She
stopped her wiping and slumped onto a chair.
"Heavens!"

"Yes, under very peculiar circumstances as well. I'm still
utterly confused as to how it happened."

Annabelle watched as Biscuit squeezed through the cat
door, her green eyes fixed upon the table. She hopped up
onto a shelf. There she sat, her tail curled around her feet,
watching the scene below as still and delicate as the orna-
mental figure of Christ beside her.

"Allow me, Philippa," Annabelle said, as she swallowed
the last of her sandwich. She took hold of the teapot and
poured some more tea into her cup. "I haven't told you the
most incredible detail yet."

Philippa leaned forward as if fearful she might miss
Annabelle's next words.

"Sir John Cartwright was *murdered*."

Philippa sat back as if thrown and gasped. She looked

incredulously around the room as if an explanation lay somewhere in Annabelle's accumulation of bric-a-brac.

"Are you sure?" she managed to say eventually.

"Fairly certain, yes."

"How ghastly! I don't believe we've ever had a murder in Upton St. Mary. It's *unimaginable*."

"I saw his body with my own eyes," Annabelle said, her hand hovering between a second sandwich and a cupcake. She settled reluctantly on the sandwich.

Annabelle continued to recount the events of the morning in as much detail as possible with all the skill of storytelling that her sermons were lauded for. Even this wasn't enough for Philippa though. The elderly woman prodded and poked with questions large and small. With all the curiosity and tenacity of a police dog, Philippa diligently went over all the inconsistencies in Annabelle's story, confirming each detail multiple times, and asking the reverend's opinion throughout.

"What of the woman?" "How young was she?" "Was she different the second time you saw her?" "How did the scream sound exactly?" "There was no sound after that?" "How long did it take you to reach the bedroom?"

Once Philippa had exhausted herself by asking questions and Annabelle by answering them, she allowed the reverend to eat a cupcake in peace. They both sat, enjoying a few moments of silence as they considered the situation in the warm, comfy atmosphere of Annabelle's kitchen.

Annabelle finished the cupcake, wiped the crumbs from her lips, and broke the silence. "Look, please don't concern yourself with this, Philippa. It's in the capable hands of Inspector Nicholls now, and I'm sure he'll find the awful creature who committed this sin eventually."

"Yes, Annabelle," Philippa said, gazing at her teacup absently, "but I was just trying to remember something."

"Yes?"

"Who in the village is a capable archer?"

"That was just one of the many questions I was hoping to answer," replied Annabelle, standing up from the table and fixing her cassock in the mirror hung beside the window. "Regardless, let's put this horrid affair aside for now. Life goes on, even in the presence of death and evil. Tomorrow's Sunday, and all this fuss has given me no time at all to prepare my sermon."

"Right, I'll leave you to it. I've yet to call the carpenter about that rickety pew."

"Oh. That's not fixed yet?"

"Unfortunately not, Annabelle," Philippa said, picking the china from the table and putting it in the sink. "Ah, Reverend?"

"Yes?" Annabelle said, turning around.

Philippa picked up the tray of cupcakes and presented them to Annabelle. "You know, you're welcome to take cupcakes whenever you wish."

Annabelle shot Philippa a look of confusion, then chuckled in bemusement. "Why, yes, Philippa. Of course."

"I mean, there's no need for you to hide your love of cakes from me!" Philippa said, laughing nervously.

"Don't worry, I won't. Whatever is the matter, Philippa?"

"Oh, nothing, Annabelle. I just think, perhaps, you're a little stressed. Nothing to be concerned about. For now."

Annabelle looked at her church secretary deeply befuddled as she sought to make sense of her strange behavior. On a day that seemed full of odd and unusual occurrences, however, she decided to reserve her critical faculties for the more concerning matters at hand. She bid Philippa a cheery farewell and made her way to the church to work on her upcoming sermon.

CHAPTER ELEVEN

JUST AS ANNABELLE expected, news of Sir John Cartwright's death spread throughout the village rapidly. She would have confided the extraordinary events to Philippa regardless but Annabelle was aware of the added benefit to be gained from Philippa's need to gossip. She had often joked that Philippa was faster at spreading both information and misinformation than the internet. Just as Inspector Nicholls would use the tools available to him to his advantage, Annabelle would use hers, in this case, the village's own little Hermes, messenger of the heavens, Philippa Bradshaw. Annabelle was certain that many of the rumors flying around about Cartwright were poppycock, but if there were any kernels of truth in them, news of his death would bring them to the fore.

As she expected, fueled by the absence of excitement that typically accompanied the sleepy Cornish weekend, the news spread to every corner of Upton St. Mary. Within a matter of hours almost every resident had not only heard of Sir John's death but had come up with multiple motives, many expositions on how the murder had been committed, and a few had even solved it!

"These rich types are all the same," grumbled a voice from the back of the *Dog and Duck*. "Always involved in something shady. Drugs, theft, you name it. Always on the make. Then, when they're getting close to being caught, they come down here, bringing trouble with them."

"Come on," pleaded a younger, less cynical voice at the bar, "there are lots of rich folk around here. Not all of them are involved in sketchy dealings."

"Yeah, but I never liked that John Cartwright. He looked shifty."

"You never even met him!" came the reply, causing a round of rowdy laughter.

"Exactly. Show me an Englishman who moves to an area whose first order of business isn't to visit his local pub, and I'll show you someone not to be trusted," replied the old grump. Laughter turned into murmurs of agreement at this distinctly British logic.

At the local playground, a couple of young mothers sitting on a bench watching their children play were just as opinionated.

"Good riddance, I say."

"Helen!"

"Well, I'm sorry, Julia, but do you really want an old pervert living this close to Upton St. Mary? They say there was some right old carry-ons going on."

"Well, we don't really know what he was doing."

"Of course we do! He was up to no good."

"You believe that?"

"Why not? We're close enough to the cities to keep the big smoke convenient and just far enough away to keep things secret. This is a great location for criminal activity!

And with that big house tucked away behind those trees, it's perfect. Why would you choose to live there if you weren't doing something shameful?"

"I suppose."

"No doubt about it. No doubt at all."

"It's not that what worries me though. The really scary thing is that there's a killer right here in Upton St. Mary. Can you imagine? How could someone *do* that? Kill someone in cold blood. It sends shivers up my spine."

"Are you talking about the grizzly werewolf?" came a chirpy voice beside the two women.

"Tommy! Don't creep up on us like that! Look, there's no werewolf. Don't talk nonsense."

"There is. The one that killed that old man."

The women exchanged glances. "Who did you hear that from?"

"Eddie told me. He said the werewolf ran into the old man's house and slashed him—like this!" Tommy swiped his curled hand through the air. "He was so strong that he left his claw sticking out of the man's chest. And the blood was going everywhere—like this!" Tommy mimicked spurts of blood shooting from his chest like geysers, falling to the ground as he did so and tossing himself around in a manner that demonstrated he was thoroughly enjoying himself.

"Come on now, Tommy. There are no werewolves around here. People would have seen them."

"Not this one. This one is clever. He disguised himself as Annabelle!"

And so it went—a game of Chinese whispers that had been played in similar villages around the globe since the dawn of communication. In some reports, the murderer was a Robin Hood-type who ransacked the home of an evil organized crime patriarch and distributed his ill-gotten gains to those in need. These needy people lived somewhere other than the village, of course, because no one in Upton St. Mary had been such a recipient. In others, the murderer was a cold-blooded killer who had conducted the act with calculated malice and who would strike again unless the villagers barricaded their windows and doors against the fearsome predator. No one thought Sir John merely unlucky or innocent of wrong-doing. Scenarios of every sort were put forth, and the lack of facts allowed a wide range of theories to flourish, most of them fanciful. After all, Sir John Cartwright had been an unknown entity while alive and was now very much a stranger in death.

Annabelle had to concede that unleashing the news of the murder on the village hadn't achieved anything, but had provided a good deal of entertainment.

CHAPTER TWELVE

SUNDAY ROLLED AROUND, and with it, Holy Communion. Despite delivering a sermon that focused on what the proverbs had to say about gossip and the judgment of neighbors, Annabelle still fielded plenty of inquisitive remarks as the congregation sidled down the well-worn steps of the church after the service.

"It's terrible, what happened, is it not, Annabelle?"

"I do hope you weren't too shaken, Reverend. I wouldn't know what to do had I been in your shoes."

"These are dark times. I do hope this horrid business blows over shortly."

Annabelle clasped her congregation's hands and reciprocated their good wishes, revealing none of her inner turmoil. Though outwardly she displayed her typical good-humor, Annabelle's mind had been twisting and turning the events of the previous day like she was trying to unlock a puzzle box. If only she could find the mechanism and unlock it to reveal the truth.

Once those who lingered had made their way out of the

church gates, Annabelle sighed deeply and joined Philippa inside.

"That was an excellent service, Annabelle. Just what the village needed," Philippa said, as she swept the aisle of the church.

"I don't suppose it'll have much of an effect, Philippa. From what I've gathered, it seems most of the village is engaged in hearsay too fantastical to bear any truth."

"Oh, I wouldn't be too sure of that," Philippa remarked ominously. "You never know what might come forth."

"Well, anyhow, I need to take my mind off this for a while. It's been consuming my thoughts since yesterday. I'll be with the bees in the orchard if you need me."

"Don't worry yourself, Annabelle. It's a lovely day to be outside. I'll have the Sunday roast on the table at 1."

Annabelle left the church, changed into her gardening shoes and protective helmet, and began tending her bees. She enjoyed her hobby greatly, consistently filled with wonder at the brightly colored insects' combination of wild abandon and symmetrical order. It also gave her an excuse to talk her thoughts out loud. She'd always found bees a most satisfying audience.

"Just look at you all! So ordered, so focused. Truly God's creatures. If only human affairs were so simple and clear. Well, I suppose it's my own fault for fancying myself as some kind of detective. I should just leave everything to the professionals. Some things should be left to higher powers. So, enough! I'll abstain from anything to do with this dastardly business. That's all I..."

Out of the corner of her eye, Annabelle saw a dark blue blue car quietly pull into the churchyard and park beside her Mini. She had only to glimpse the inspector's brush-like hair before she was scampering to greet him.

"Ah, Reverend!" Inspector Nicholls said.

"Inspector! So lovely to see you!"

"And you," he said, casting his eyes over her outfit.

Annabelle snorted as she frantically pulled off her gardening gloves to shake his hand.

"I hope I wasn't interrupting you," the inspector said.

"Oh, not at all. I was just tending my bees." The inspector squinted and strained to hear her. Her voice was muffled and she suddenly remembered that she was wearing her bee-keeping helmet. She removed it quickly and tossed her hair into place in a manner she hoped wasn't too glamorous for a vicar.

"You keep bees?"

"Yes. It's a silly hobby, I know, but it passes the time."

"I don't think it's silly. I think it's rather interesting."

"Yes, yes it is, isn't it?" Annabelle breathed.

They smiled at each other awkwardly for a few moments before the inspector said, "I was just on my way to the crime scene, so I thought I'd drop by and see how you were doing. You seemed a little... flustered, yesterday."

"Oh, well, I wasn't at my best," laughed Annabelle. "I'm much better now. Thank you for asking, Inspector."

"I thought you seemed to take finding a murder victim rather well. The last time I spoke to someone who had discovered a dead body, they were covered in their own vomit."

Annabelle laughed so loudly that Philippa appeared to see what all the fuss was about. Catching sight of her, Annabelle promptly flicked her hand in a peculiar gesture intended to send Philippa away, a gesture she hoped the inspector wouldn't notice.

"Are you alright, Reverend?" The inspector looked puzzled by Annabelle's jerking movements.

"Yes, inspector. I think I have a bee sting on my hand."

"Oh, let me see."

As the inspector leaned over and took Annabelle's hand, she struggled to stay upright. Philippa, who had ignored Annabelle's efforts to leave the pair in peace was still looking over at them. She winked at Annabelle, enjoying the scene. With the inspector peering intensely at Annabelle's hand as he looked in vain for a bee sting, she mouthed the word "Shoo!" at her church secretary and waved her hand in the air as aggressively as she could over the head of the inspector. Philippa shrugged and threw up her hands, smiling. She made no attempt to move.

"I can't see anything, but I suppose they don't swell up until much later. Perhaps you should put some ice on it," the inspector said, finally giving up his investigation.

"Precisely, Inspector. Thank you." Annabelle gave a little bob, grateful that he hadn't seemed to notice the drama between her and Philippa.

Nicholls looked around at the churchyard, the orchard, and cottage garden. He nodded his appreciation. "You've got a nice setup here. I should let you get back to your bees."

"Inspector, have you made any progress? Into the murder, I mean. Have you looked into Sir John Cartwright's background, at all?"

The inspector's face stiffened. "Yes."

"And was there anything peculiar about him? I ask, because he's still very much a mystery to the village residents. They imagine all sorts of things. I'm sure they are making it up to fill a vacuum."

"Well, I wouldn't normally say this to someone outside the investigation," said the inspector. He leaned toward Annabelle conspiratorially, making her heart flutter and causing her to breathe more deeply to calm herself. "But he was well known to the police in London."

"Oh?"

"He'd been under suspicion for several years, though never charged, of running an escort agency, money laundering, possibly drugs. He was quite a sort."

CHAPTER THIRTEEN

"**G**OLLY GOSH!" Annabelle cried.

"INDEED. Not the sort of thing you usually hear about in a place like Upton St. Mary is it?" Inspector Nicholls replied.

"No... I mean, yes... I mean..." Annabelle trailed off and looked into the distance.

"Reverend?"

"Inspector, remember the rumors I told you about?"

"Of course."

"Well, that's almost exactly *it*. I thought it was utter nonsense. People watching too many television shows, but I suppose there was some truth to the rumors after all."

"Truth to what? I'm not following, Reverend."

Annabelle took a deep breath before continuing. "People were saying all manner of things about him, much of it complete poppycock. But one of the things that kept cropping up was this idea that Cartwright had moved into *Woodlands Manor* with the intent of turning it into some sort of party palace."

"I see," said the inspector, nodding gently.

"I suppose someone had heard about his past, and that's where the gossip began. But I never expected there to be any truth to it. It seems so implausible."

"Well, Reverend, when you've done this job for as long as I have, you learn just how unbelievable the truth can turn out to be."

"But a *Sir*? Drugs? Money laundering? Prostitution? I wonder how he got into it?"

"My guess would be he fell into it. A respected member of high society looking for a bit of excitement. Trusted. He's the guy you'd want to buy from if you're into that sort of thing. He saw a gap in the market and decided to fill it, as it were." The inspector held up his hand in apology. "Sorry, Reverend. I don't mean to sound crude."

"Oh, of course not," giggled Annabelle, "I may be a person of the cloth, but I'm not a prude. Uh, I mean... Not that I approve of such things... Well, the paying part. That's the part I disapprove of... Not the... But then..." Annabelle stammered, before deciding to stop digging. She got herself back on topic. "Do you think that he was really planning to open some kind of den of iniquity here in Upton St. Mary? Or was it an escape from all that? I mean, he was *meditating* when he was killed."

The inspector sucked air through his teeth. "Not sure. If he was, we could pretty much pin a motive on every member of the village and half the London underworld. On the other hand, if you were looking to make a fresh start, I can't think of any other place better than Upton St. Mary."

"Indeed."

"Did you hear anything else as you went around your parish?"

"No, only a story about a werewolf getting him."

The inspector laughed. The sound set Annabelle's

heart aflutter again. "Well, I never rule anything out!" he said.

They chuckled together for a few moments before the inspector reached into the deep pocket of his trench coat and pulled out a folded piece of paper.

"Since you're officially a member of the investigation team now..."

"Really?" exclaimed Annabelle.

"Just a joke," the inspector carefully assured her.

"Oh."

"But since you're so interested in the details, you might want to know that I received the autopsy report this morning." He handed Annabelle the sheet of paper. "Nothing surprising. He was in good health, as you'd expect from a man who meditates. Died from a lacerated lung and heart failure brought on by a serious puncture wound. It confirms the time of death. Just as Harper predicted, he died well before you found him. So that's the easy explanation gone; that the scream came from Sir John himself."

Annabelle perused the report, nodding her head from time to time to make it seem like she understood its contents.

"I see," she said, after a full two minutes. She handed the sheet back to the inspector.

"Well," he sighed, "I've dilly-dallied long enough. I should be off."

"Of course, Inspector. Sorry for keeping you."

"No problem. You've given me more help than you realize. Be careful, Reverend. There are some nasty people about."

The inspector got into his car and waved at Annabelle as he backed out of his space and trundled through the gates to the road.

"See you soon!" shouted Annabelle, but he was already gone.

She turned on her heels to return to her bees to find Philippa standing right in front of her, a wry grin deepening the wrinkles that crisscrossed her face.

CHAPTER FOURTEEN

THE WOMAN WHO sat in the tea room on the second floor of the Athenaeum Hotel projected an aura of movie-star glamor and refined taste. Her cream-colored pencil skirt was stretched tight across the contours of her hips and thighs and she tapped one of her pastel blue, high-heeled stilettos against the other. She turned her head elegantly toward the window, her sapphire blue eyes peering indifferently down her small nose at the London traffic. With her blond hair pinned up into a tight bun, she cut a statuesque, polished figure as precisely engineered and effortlessly timeless as the leather upholstery and regal pillars of the luxurious tea room. The woman extended her long, slender fingers to pick up a delicately sculpted teacup and brought it to her crimson lips, sipping silently before replacing the cup quietly with a deft, graceful movement.

As if sensing the presence of her guest, she cast her eyes toward the room's entrance and saw a woman pass under the chandelier that hung from the ceiling. Though not as slim or as tall as the seated figure, this new woman showed just as much decorum, seeming to glide over the soft carpet in black shoes that perfectly complemented her bright red dress. The woman in the red dress eased herself into a leather chair opposite the woman in the cream skirt. No greetings were exchanged, the two of them trading wry smirks, the only acknowledgment friends of many decades and frequent meetings needed. The newcomer had a dark complexion. Her brown, almond-shaped eyes and black-brown hair cascaded in waves around her shoulders. She tossed her head gently with the haughtiness of a finely bred racehorse, causing glimmers of light to ripple and settle along the silky curves of her mane.

"Did you come to take tea," said the first woman, nodding subtly toward the ample cleavage revealed by the second's dress, "or to seduce it?"

"Inner beauty is of no use," replied the other, "unless you reveal it on occasion."

As their smiles grew, the woman in the red dress gestured a waiter over. He was a smartly dressed man in his twenties, well used to the manners and strong personalities of the Athenaeum's élite clientele. But even he felt daunted in the presence of such formidable and sharp women. Despite their easy demeanor and class, they exuded a dangerous and pointed energy that was intimidating to those who couldn't match their wits. After taking their order, he spun on his heel and returned to the tea bar as quickly as he could, before they found and exploited any point of weakness.

"You may wish you had ordered something a little stronger, dear Sophie. Something unpalatable has occurred. I'm still struggling to digest it myself," the woman in the pencil skirt said. She picked up a newspaper from the table and with a flick of her wrist, handed it to her companion.

Sophie took the newspaper and read it in the pale morning light that poured through the thick panes of the window next to which they were sitting.

"John Cartwright is dead?" she stated. She tossed the newspaper on the table and looked steadily ahead at her companion.

"Murdered. By an archer."

"What a to-do. It's positively Shakespearean."

"It's why I prefer my knights in shining armor."

"I didn't know archers still roamed these shores?"

"In abundance. I am a persistent target of darting glances."

"If knights can still exist in this day and age, I suppose archers can, too."

"Despite chivalry being well and truly, utterly dead."

They tittered gently as the waiter brought Sophie's order, and with a quick nod of thanks, he was sent on his way.

"This is a cause for concern though, Gabriella. What of our investment?" asked Sophie, bringing her voice down a notch.

"I was just considering it," replied her friend, tapping thin fingers against her chair's armrest. "Our aim must be to avoid any losses."

Sophie nodded, then shook her lustrous hair and pressed a finger against her full lips. "The situation appears to be very much unknown, however. No suspect. No conviction."

"Indeed. Not to mention peculiar. Especially for such a quaint and traditional village such as Upton St. Mary."

"In which mild-mannered residents are no doubt in a state of unrest and confusion at this outlandish occurrence," Sophie quipped, drolly.

Their eyes lit up as they simultaneously sipped from their teacups. After a few moments, Gabriella's lips formed a slow, feline-like smile. "I do believe we are, as ever, thinking the same thing, my dear Sophie," she said.

"That affairs of murder and conspiracy deserve an attention that is best *not* left to the gentle, kind people who reside in that Arcadian corner of the kingdom known as Cornwall?"

"But to a pair that have a vested interest in the successful outcome of said affair. And that this pair would be best served in their endeavors by entering the sleepy village stealthily and undercover."

Sophie's eyes widened, and she leaned forward in glee. "Are you suggesting, dearest Gabriella, a little game of dress-up?"

"You know too well, Sophie, that I need only the slightest excuse."

"It would certainly allow us to ease into the daily rituals of village life and discover everything we can from the villagers."

"Absolutely. It is the most efficient way for us to endeavor to secure our investment," Gabriella said.

"And with which type of sheep's clothing should we adorn ourselves?"

"Why it's obvious, is it not? Two wealthy women visiting a deliciously British village, invading the privacy of others with an unseemly curiosity."

"Tourists!" they said, in near-perfect unison.

They laughed, Sophie's musical, rich tone offering a perfect counterpoint to Gabriella's delicately high-pitched giggles. "Where shall we claim to be tourists from?" Gabriella pondered.

"An interesting question," replied Sophie, pursing her lips as she considered the options. "Germany?"

"Darling, my fashion sense is far too good. How about Italian?"

"I certainly have the look," said Sophie, tossing her thick, dark hair. "But I struggle to imagine why an Italian would be interested in any other place on Earth."

"True," replied Gabriella. "Australians, perhaps?"

"I don't drink nearly enough," Sophie said, "and I prefer not to wear a backpack *any*where. Russian, maybe."

"No, no. The aim is to *deflect* attention, not attract it."

"Americans?" Sophie put forward, cautiously.

"Too stereotypical. Besides, people would assume we'd just been waylaid on the way to Paris or London."

"Well, how about French?"

Gabriella pondered for a few moments, before turning back toward Sophie and nodding slightly. "Yes. I do speak French, after all."

"It would provide the perfect opportunity to ravish our wardrobes," Sophie added.

"And establish our credentials as exotic femme fatales."

"Good," Sophie said. "It's settled."

"*Allez!*"

CHAPTER FIFTEEN

TRY AS SHE might, Annabelle could not take her mind off the murder of Sir John Cartwright. Since the inspector's visit and his disclosure of Cartwright's background, she had tried hard to keep her hands and mind busy. She threw herself into her weekend routine: tending to her bees, preparing her sermon, and doing her very best to persuade Biscuit to play with her. Unfortunately, in distracting herself and in provoking Biscuit's interest, she failed miserably.

"Oh, do come on, Biscuit! Look! I've bought you a brand new toy! Surely you're tempted to at least sniff it," she said in a sing-songy voice, dangling a ball in front of the ginger cat's thousand-yard stare as she sat in the middle of Annabelle's living room floor. "It's even got catnip in it!"

"There's no playing with that cat," came Philippa's voice as she gathered her coat, ready to leave having just dropped off the church's cleaning rota. "She does everything on her terms. Always has, always will."

"Come on, girl! Don't be shy!" persisted Annabelle.

"I'll see you tomorrow, Reverend," Philippa called. She closed the door behind her.

"Bye, Philippa!" Annabelle turned her attention back to the orange tabby in front of her. "No? Perhaps if I just leave the toy in front of you," Annabelle said, placing the ball in front of Biscuit's tiny paws. "I'll just go into the other room and leave you to investigate it."

Annabelle walked across the living room out of sight of Biscuit and stamped her feet a few times loudly on the floor. She counted to ten, then peeked slowly around the door-frame hoping to find Biscuit joyfully pawing at her new purchase. But no, Biscuit merely looked up at Annabelle, as apparently disinterested in her as she was with the ball that lay untouched at her feet.

"That's it!" Annabelle exclaimed, grabbing her hat and gloves. "You're no fun at all. I'm off. I'm of more importance to the inspector than I am to you." Annabelle threw on her favorite red and black-checkered coat and grabbed her keys. "Oh, and Philippa is right, you are becoming terribly fat!" she said. In a huff, she locked the front door and marched over to her car.

Annabelle drove without pleasure, her questions regarding the murder only intensifying as she thought about them. She liked things clear, ordered, proper—and so far nothing about the horrific death of Sir John Cartwright was as she liked it.

The stormy weather of her thoughts was so intoxicating that as she drove along the long driveway to *Woodlands Manor*, she almost failed to notice the driver of the car heading in her direction. The car pulled over to let her pass. It stopped on the grassy verge and a man wound down his window. Annabelle's mood quickly cleared.

"Hello, Inspector!" she said

"Hello, Reverend. Surprised to see you here."

"I just thought I'd drop by to see if a visit might jog any important memories I might have forgotten in all the fuss."

"Good idea." The inspector nodded. "But the house is all locked up now. We've been looking over the crime scene again. The SOCO team has been and gone. I'm the last to leave. I might come back tomorrow, but I don't see a reason to at present."

"Have you discovered anything new?"

Mike Nicholls sighed. "Nothing too extraordinary. Apparently, the arrow that killed the victim didn't come from an ordinary bow."

"Oh?"

"It came from a crossbow."

"Oh dear. Those things are the devil," said Annabelle.

"Yeah. It also throws off our projections regarding the position the murderer shot from. Crossbows are more accurate than simple, straightforward bows. The shooter could have been standing anywhere."

"That's strange," mused Annabelle.

"How so?" the inspector asked.

"Well, archery with a regular bow and arrow is a fairly well-practiced sport in this area. It would make a lot of sense to assume that was the weapon. But I've not heard of a crossbow used anywhere locally."

The inspector chuckled grimly. "It seems like this case just gets harder rather than easier."

Annabelle bid the inspector farewell. He rolled his window back up and drove off, leaving Annabelle to close in on the fountain that had by now become a familiar sight.

As she got out of the Mini and began making her way around the house, Annabelle mulled over an idea she had stopped short of telling the inspector. Archery was a popular pastime in and around the village. As a predominantly male-oriented sport, archery skills were often passed down from father to son, a popular excuse for some male bonding between generations. It was unlikely that somewhere along the line, the community of close-knit archers had suddenly embraced the crossbow—a much more brutal and ugly weapon that required none of the finesse or skill of the traditional bow.

It was entirely possible, of course, that someone in the village had recently taken it up, but news of that hadn't reached Annabelle's ears. She had visited almost all of the homes in the village at one time or other and seen many a proud huntsman display his fine weapons on a mantel or in a wall frame. She had observed the camouflage-clad hunters setting off for a day of hunting in the early hours, bearing weapons across their backs. Not once had she seen any of them use, own, or even mention a crossbow. This led her to a conclusion that was at the same time both unnerving and comforting; the murderer must have come from outside the village.

As she turned a corner and found herself at the rear of the big house, Annabelle looked back and was struck by another thought. The murderer may not have planned it!

She noticed that all the windows, including the one at which Sir John was meditating, were now closed. The windows presented an obvious obstacle to a successful murder attempt. No matter how thunderous a shot, the trajectory would have been too unpredictable for the murderer to have successfully shot through glass. That meant the murderer *needed* the window to be open to carry out the killing.

Annabelle thought about this. While the murderer might have known Sir John Cartwright liked to meditate in front of open windows, a slightly chilly day or rain would have scuppered his plans. Perhaps the murderer had visited the site day after day, waiting for the perfect circumstances to present themselves—Sir John's eyes-closed meditation, an open window, and no onlookers. But Annabelle found that unlikely given that Sir John had only lived at *Woodlands Manor* for a few days. No, as Annabelle considered this, she began to believe that the murderer was an opportunist. The death might even have been an accident!

It wasn't a big lead or even a watertight theory but Annabelle felt she had the slimmest of threads to follow. She had been reluctant to tell the inspector her idea that the killer was an outsider. She feared she sounded ridiculous. But she could investigate quietly without telling anyone.

Annabelle turned her attention to the rough ground where the dense woods met the manicured lawns at the rear of the house. She stepped forward carefully, intently searching every peculiar stone and suspicious mound for something tangible. After exploring for a whole hour and feeling the oncoming chill of evening starting to settle, Annabelle turned back toward the house. Despite the fruit-lessness of her search, she resolved to come back, hope stirring in her that with enough effort she would find the key to this particularly vexing puzzle.

CHAPTER SIXTEEN

OVER THE NEXT few days, Annabelle returned to the large manor house several times. She came equipped with a set of binoculars and a moleskin notepad in which she scribbled anything she considered useful. Before her second "expedition," she called Harper Jones and quizzed the pathologist on everything she knew. After the briefest of explanations as to why Annabelle was calling her, Harper was surprisingly forthcoming with enough details to fill an entire page of the reverend's notebook. They were all technical and complicated, however. Math had been a favorite subject of Annabelle's, but even she struggled to understand more than half of the calculations and measurements Harper offered her. Despite this, Annabelle persisted. As she traipsed through the woods, armed with a flask of tea under one arm and her binoculars strung around her neck, she tried her very best to triangulate from where the murderer had fired the fatal shot.

Despite imagining herself on the trail of a cold-blooded killer, Annabelle couldn't help but enjoy herself. She loved hearing birdsong and was in awe of the majesty of the trees. She found herself frequently bending over to observe the beauty of a butterfly or a spider weaving a silvery, intricate web. She felt herself relax and focus. Apart from a slight scare when something rustled in some nearby bushes, the hours she spent in the woods were good for her soul, if not her investigation. And yet, while she felt that she was getting closer to the truth, Harper's calculations still proved too abstract for her, and each time Annabelle left, she felt slightly disappointed.

She was no less determined, however, and the next day Annabelle again packed her binoculars and her notebook in preparation for a few hours reconnaissance. This time, she took a small detour on her way to *Woodlands Manor*. Mr. Squires was one of the keenest archers in Upton St. Mary and one of the most trustworthy people Annabelle knew. He was an elderly gentleman who always wore clothes in deep forest green. He had a thick, grey mustache that gave him the air of an old wartime general and when he invited Annabelle into his office, she saw it was adorned with old leather-bound books and watercolor paintings of various hunting scenes. After asking for his discretion, Annabelle showed him Harper's calculations and the dimensions of the crime scene.

For a little over an hour, Mr. Squires regaled Annabelle on archery, crossbows, and distance-power ratios. He troubled to give her full explanations of all the factors involved including wind, weights, the kind of arrows used, and the skill required. His explanations were comprehensive and Annabelle left him feeling extremely grateful and knowing more than she ever needed or intended to know about the centuries-old pastime.

When she found herself back in the woods, Annabelle

applied everything she had learned, taking great care to incorporate all the information she had gathered. After carefully cross-checking her notes multiple times and making many fine adjustments, she finally found herself standing a few dozen yards away from the edge of the woods. She was on an incline, surrounded by a handful of trees that hid her almost completely but also afforded her a clear view and a straight shot—right into Sir John Cartwright's window.

"This has to be it!" she exclaimed as she checked her calculations again to make sure she had made no mistakes. "This is where he—or she—must have stood when he—or she—fired the shot." She tamped at the ground with her foot. "It certainly *feels* like a murderer's spot." It was an area of the woods that would be perfect if one wanted to hide. Annabelle felt a shiver run up her spine. "Don't be silly, old girl."

Then came a sound. It was a rustle, similar to the kind Annabelle had heard the day before and which she had assumed to come from a small woodland animal. Standing there, where a few days previously one person had ended the life of another, the sound took on an ominous weight. Annabelle crouched and stayed as silent as possible, her ears alert to any sounds. Once again, the bushes rustled. Annabelle's blood rushed through her body and she gripped her flask tightly in one hand, her crucifix in the other.

She turned around slowly, looking for the source of the sound. As she rotated in almost a complete circle, the sound came again from directly behind her. Only this time it didn't stop. Annabelle spun so quickly toward it that she slipped on the soft soil and tumbled backward. She shut her eyes and screamed as the rustling grew so loud it was now mere inches away from her. "Our father, who art in heaven, hallowed be thy name..." Annabelle muttered, quickly and quietly, until she felt something press against her leg. She opened her eyes in horror. "Biscuit!"

"Meow."

Annabelle stared at her cat, startled into silence. She reached out and stroked the cat's head, as if unable to believe the source of her terror was none other than the church cat. Biscuit pressed her head against Annabelle's hand. "What on earth are you doing so far from the church? We're almost two miles away!"

Annabelle picked up the cat and cuddled her to her chest. Biscuit licked her face, causing Annabelle to double-check that the cat she held in her arms was actually Biscuit. "I do believe all this drama is driving me quite mad and more than a little hungry. I want one of Philippa's cupcakes so badly I can smell them," Annabelle joked, as she placed the cat on the ground, stood up, and brushed off her slacks.

After adjusting her clothes, Annabelle picked up her notebook from the dirt and tucked it away into her pocket. She clipped her flask to her waistband and looked down at the damp, moss-covered floor of the woods. "I suppose we'll have to look for clues together now, Biscuit," she said.

Heavy rainfall the previous night had soaked the earth, flattening it. The only markings Annabelle could see were her own footprints. As she carefully walked back and forth, desperately seeking something that would offer a clue as to the murderer's identity, her heart sank.

"Oh, Biscuit, I'm starting to think all my efforts have been for naught," Annabelle sighed. "Although I think I know where the murderer was when he fired the shot. The inspector will be interested in knowing that, won't he, Biscuit?" Annabelle glanced around. Biscuit had disappeared. "Biscuit? *Biscuit?*" she said, rushing forward. She turned her head once more and noticed the tabby cat crouching next to the two trees between which the crossbow's arrow must have flown. Annabelle looked up. Darkness was falling. "I think it's time we went home. Come on."

Biscuit, however, was not yet ready to leave. The ginger cat began pawing at the ground. Annabelle waited patiently for her to finish. She looked toward the house and the window Sir John had been meditating beneath, then back at the cat. This time, Annabelle noticed something sticking out of the earth.

"What's this? What have you found, Biscuit?" she said, gently nudging the cat aside and pulling something from the ground. Annabelle rubbed the dirt away and peered closely at it. Her shoulders slumped in disappointment. A cigarette butt. How would that help? A moment from tossing it away, however, she paused.

In her now numerous trips to the woods, she hadn't noticed rubbish of any kind, let alone signs of cigarettes. The men of the village were as proud of the woods as their wives were of their homes, and they did their utmost to keep them unspoiled. No villager would have left behind any kind of litter. It was ingrained in them since childhood to leave the countryside as they found it. A stranger had left behind this butt. And it lay at the *precise* spot where the murderer fired his shot.

Annabelle studied the cigarette end further, noticing how fresh and clean it looked. She placed it carefully into her pocket, picked Biscuit up, and strode purposefully back toward her car. Her investigation was deepening. It was bearing fruit.

CHAPTER SEVENTEEN

I T WAS ALMOST dark by the time Annabelle got home. The village by night was a serene place. Lights in cottage windows twinkled like the stars in the clear night sky. Except for raucous bouts of laughter and occasional music from the pub, silence hung in the air like a heavy blanket. You could hear owl calls for miles.

Annabelle got out of her Mini, quickly followed by Biscuit. The cat disappeared into the shadows to conduct her nightly affairs. Annabelle walked into the warmth of her kitchen. "A cup of tea and bed for me," Annabelle said, with a sigh. It had been a long day.

Just as she was removing her coat, however, the phone rang. Annabelle closed her eyes and groaned. She picked up the receiver. "Hello?"

"Hello, Annabelle." It was Philippa. "It's rather late, Philippa. Is something wrong?"

"Not at all, Annabelle," Philippa said, a little too brightly. "I just wanted to see how you were."

"Oh, well, thank you. I'm rather pleased, actually. I think I've got some new information on the murder."

"Don't concern yourself so much with that, Reverend. It's a job for the professionals. You already push yourself too hard."

"I appreciate your thoughts, Philippa. But really, I'm absolutely fine. I'll rest well and good once the murderer has been caught."

"I'm sure you will, Annabelle. I'm sure you will."

"Thank you, Philippa. Is that all?" There was a pause. Annabelle waited.

"I was reading this article, Annabelle," Philippa blurted out.

Annabelle rolled her eyes. This conversation was not going to end soon. "What article was that?"

"It was about kleptomania. Do you know what that is, Annabelle?"

"I'm not sure I do, Philippa," replied Annabelle, her defenses rising as she prepared to be schooled by her church secretary.

"It's a disease. A psychological *confliction*. It's where someone is compelled to steal things for no other reason than to steal them. And then lie about it."

"That sounds dreadful," Annabelle said. "But why ever would you ask me about that? Do you know someone who has this... *affliction?*"

"Oh... ah... yes, maybe I do."

"That's awful. I'm deeply sorry to hear that."

"What do you think I should do, Annabelle?"

"Well, stealing is a sin, of course. But if this... *person* is doing so because of an illness, well, I should think the most Christian thing would be to show compassion and to forgive them."

"Hmm," said Philippa. "I had a feeling you would say that."

"Would you like me to speak to the person?"

"No, no, Annabelle. That would be rather difficult. Thank you, that's all."

"Okay, well, see you tomorrow, and sleep tight."

"You too, Annabelle."

Annabelle hung up the phone and prepared for bed. As she cleaned her teeth, she wondered why investigating a murder was more straightforward than talking to Philippa. Her church secretary could be confounding at times.

CHAPTER EIGHTEEN

TIME PASSED in the village of Upton St. Mary much the same as it always had—filled with simple pleasures and satisfying, dependable routines. But talk of the murder showed no sign of abating. With much of the village still in the dark as to the nature of the killing as well as the killer, the joys of speculation still had plenty of mileage. When Annabelle told the inspector what she had discovered and gave him the cigarette butt, he was almost lost for words even if his countenance remained professional. Annabelle was ecstatic. Philippa always had told her that "the way to a man's heart is helping him do his job better!"

"How are the other parts of the investigation going, Inspector?"

Nicholls pursed his lips. "I'll share something with you, Reverend, but I'd appreciate it if you kept it to yourself."

"Of course, Inspector!" Annabelle was delighted to be taken into the detective's confidence.

"It's been almost two weeks now. I'm beginning to worry the trail is going cold. If you're right, and the killer is a stranger to these parts, then he—or she—could be anywhere by now." He held up the cigarette stub Annabelle had given him. "This is a breakthrough. We can run DNA tests on this cigarette, but we are at a critical stage. The longer we go without a clear suspect, the harder it will be to solve the crime."

He seemed down but Annabelle was her usual irrepressible, enthusiastic self. "Oh come, come, Inspector. I don't share your pessimism. I'm sure the key to the murder is just within reach. We'll solve this crime. How can we not? We have God on our side. "

The open-top Jaguar's slinky curves reflected the trees and hedgerows that whipped past as it hurtled down the country lanes toward Upton St. Mary. At the wheel joyfully guiding the car, her hair flowing magnificently behind her was Sophie. The long, lithe form of Gabriella was stretched out in the passenger seat, an arm nonchalantly hanging out of the window, another clutching a purple beret to her head.

Sophie drove the car around what looked like the ruins of a castle and brought the car to a slow stop to allow a farmer and his sheep across the road. She winked at the farmer. Unused to such gestures, he raised his eyebrows but smiled as he urged his sheep forward.

"Such a spiritual part of the world, isn't it?" Sophie said, as she watched the bleating sheep who were bulked up with wool and in need of a good shearing stagger across the lane.

"Unquestionably," replied Gabriella, "I've often considered making a home in the country."

"*You?*" exclaimed Sophie. "I find it difficult to imagine you living anywhere further than two miles of Harrods."

"Harrods isn't going anywhere. London is always nearby, wherever in the world you are. Especially these days when you can get anything you want with the press of a button."

"And what, pray tell, would a lady of such sophistication and fine tastes *do* in this rural paradise?"

Gabriella gazed upward. "I'm sure I could make my own entertainment. If it's good enough for the Queen, it might just do for me. Clean air and fresh, local produce is wonderful for the skin, too."

"And who would I call upon for tea when you are gone?"

"Oh, darling! I'd take you with me, of course. I shall probably require a milkmaid!"

"How incredibly cheeky of you!" grinned Sophie, as she put the car in first gear and drove away after the last sheep had crossed into the neighboring field. The farmer saluted his thanks.

Eventually, the two women arrived in the village and like travelers of old, were almost magnetically drawn to its highest, most visible, point—the church spire. As Sophie swept the sleek car through the narrow, cobbled village streets, they noticed smartly dressed people heading toward the church's old iron gates.

"I do believe we're in time for communion," Gabriella said.

"A church service? But we've only just arrived!"

"Why not? Churches are pillars of small communities like these. We need to find out what's going on. I can't think of a better way of ingratiating ourselves than by attending church."

Sophie raised a curious eyebrow at her friend. "You may be better suited to the country life than I suspected."

Upton St. Mary was used to tourists and visitors of many kinds but even so the two women, with their fine clothes and haughty dispositions, drew more than a few glances and whispers. The women took a pew at the very back of the church and proceeded to mouth the words to the hymns and listen intently to the female vicar's stirring sermon.

Once the service was over, they milled around with the rest of the congregation expecting to engage with whoever was curious enough to ask them who they were. They were surprised when the reverend herself made a beeline for them.

"Hello! I'm Annabelle, vicar of this fine, old place. It's always nice to receive new visitors."

"Oh," fumbled Sophie, "*Bonjour.*"

"French?" Annabelle said, before pressing a finger to her lips as she tried to remember the French classes she took at school. "Let's see. *Mon français n'est pas bon, mais je comprends un peu.*"

Sophie looked desperately at Gabriella. This was way more French than she was prepared for.

"We speak English," Gabriella said, giving her voice a slight French accent. "*C'est bon*, Reverend. You can speak English with us."

"Oh, good!" Annabelle said, clapping her hands together. "I haven't spoken French since I was a young girl! Such a beautiful language, though. I take it you are both tourists? Visitors?"

"Yes. Zis iz ze troof," Sophie spoke with an accent so forced it sounded more like a speech impediment. "We are ze tourists. There iz no miztake."

Annabelle gazed perplexed at both women. She frowned a little. Sophie glared at Gabriella again, begging her to save the moment.

"Tourists," Gabriella agreed, confidently. "With some business to do."

"I see," mused Annabelle. She was growing suspicious of these two bizarre women, one of whom spoke in an accent that was unlike any she had ever heard and the other far too self-assured to be a down-to-earth tourist, the like of which Cornwall hosted on an ongoing basis. "I take it you've just arrived?"

"*Oui*," Sophie said.

Annabelle had to know what these women wanted. "My house is just over there. I insist you join me for a spot of lunch. I'd like to do everything I can to make your visit a pleasurable and memorable one."

"Thank you so very kindly, Reverend," said Gabriella, urging her friend toward the house. "We would like that very much."

CHAPTER NINETEEN

FIFTEEN MINUTES LATER after the congregation had dispersed to their homes for Sunday lunch, or the pub, the two women found themselves sitting around the table watching Annabelle pour them hot cups of tea.

"I'm terribly sorry, I didn't catch your names," Annabelle said.

"Gabriella."

"S... So... Sophie."

"Welcome to Upton St. Mary, Gabriella and Sophie," Annabelle said, cheerfully.

Philippa burst into the room carrying plates of food. "I've prepared some sandwiches for your guests, Annabelle," she said. "I've also made some more cupcakes," she added, looking at Annabelle as she did so.

"Wonderful," said Annabelle, oblivious to Philippa's pointed words.

Sophie picked at a sandwich and took a bite. "*Magnifique!*"

After they had sipped their tea and nibbled on their

sandwiches for a bit, Annabelle casually questioned the two women. "I would be more than happy to help you enjoy our humble village in any way I can."

"Thank you, Reverend," Gabriella said.

"Please, call me Annabelle."

"Oh, zis cat is adorable!" Sophie said as Biscuit rubbed her body against Sophie's foot.

"That's Biscuit. She's actually very temperamental," Annabelle said. She struggled to hide the annoyance she felt at Biscuit giving more attention to these strangers than she ever did to her owner.

"*Belle!*"

"Perhaps I can help with this business concern you have," Annabelle said.

Gabriella glanced at Sophie. "Yes, indeed," she said. "You may be able to help us."

"Happy to," Annabelle said, warmly.

"We've learned of a business associate's passing. He lived in the area. We want to pay our respects to the family."

"I see," Annabelle said. "I'm sorry for your loss. Who was the poor soul?"

"Zir *Jean* Cartwright," Sophie said.

Annabelle spilled her tea. "Oh dear!" she sputtered. She dabbed at her cassock before excusing herself. She ran to the kitchen where Philippa was busy tidying up.

"Philippa!" she whispered, as excitedly as she could without being overheard.

"Yes, Annabelle?"

"They're here about Sir John Cartwright!" Annabelle said, pointing toward the door that led to the living room.

Philippa dropped her tea towel on the counter. "Really?"

"Yes!" Annabelle said, nodding furiously. "They say they're French tourists but there's something awfully queer about them."

Philippa ran to the door and pressed her ear to it.

"What are you doing?"

Philippa put a finger to her lips to shush Annabelle, then beckoned her over. Annabelle tip-toed to the door and carefully placed her ear against the wood.

"...respects? We would do better to find that Poppy girl, first."

"Poppy?"

"You know! The impossibly young woman that John lived with in London. There was a rumor he brought her here with him."

"But she was young enough to be his daughter!"

"Exactly. She wasn't old enough to be his friend!"

"Well, if she's here, I'm sure the vicar will take us to her."

"I hope so. She seems like a bright sort."

"Your accent wouldn't fool her even if she wasn't."

"Oh shush, so long as we can protect our investment..."

Annabelle leaped back from the door. Philippa pulled back as well.

"Did you hear that?" Annabelle hissed, struggling not to squeal her surprise.

"I knew there was something wrong with that Sir John. I told you, didn't I? Fancy that, a woman young enough to be his daughter."

"Oh Philippa, that's beside the point. These women aren't French at all! They're investors probably in some scheme cooked up with that Cartwright fellow! He was up to all sorts, you know. Out of the way, I should get back in there before they suspect something."

"Please be careful, Annabelle. They could be dangerous"

Annabelle opened the door theatrically. "I've just had a little chat with Philippa, my church secretary," she said. Philippa followed her into the room. "She would be more than happy to make arrangements for your stay in our village. There's a delightful bed-and-breakfast nearby that offers everything you could possibly need."

"Oh, zat is zo kind of you, but we do not need zis treatment."

"Please, I insist!" Annabelle said. "There's no point coming to Upton St. Mary if you can't appreciate our hospitality!"

Just before the two strangers left Annabelle's home, Annabelle pulled Philippa aside and said, "Make sure nothing they say goes further than your ears and mine. This could be the key to the entire case."

"Of course, Annabelle. I won't tell a soul," Philippa assured her.

As Annabelle merrily waved the women off, she remembered Philippa had a crochet club meeting the next day. She sighed wearily. Any information she gleaned from the women probably wouldn't stay confidential beyond Philippa's second row of chain stitch.

CHAPTER TWENTY

THE MAN WHO sat in the interview room was tall and lean. He wore a tweed waistcoat, knitted wool tie with a checked shirt, and green corduroy trousers—the uniform of the local country squire. He was jiggling his knee up and down and his wrinkled, brown, leathery face showed that he was extremely distressed. He ran his hand repeatedly through his fair, thinning hair. The door opened and Inspector Nicholls confidently entered the room. He took a seat opposite the man and laid a file on the table in front of him.

"What is this? What is…" the man said. Mike Nicholls held up a finger to silence him.

The inspector pressed a button on the tape recorder placed at the end of the table and spoke into it. "Inspector Mike Nicholls interviewing Harry Cooper. Sunday, the fourteenth of September, two thirty-four PM." He turned to his interviewee. "You are Harry Cooper, correct?"

"Y-yes."

"You formerly owned the property known as *Wood-*

lands Manor, situated just off Arden Road, near the village of Upton St. Mary?"

"Yes," Harry Cooper said, nervously. "I don't own it anymore. I sold it."

"To whom?"

"To a syndicate, the leader of which was Sir John Cartwright. Why are you asking me? You know this."

"Just answer the questions, sir. The new owner was murdered. Did you know that?"

"Yes, of course. It was in the papers."

"The owner was killed two weeks ago. Were you in or around the property on the day of the murder?"

"No! Absolutely not! I haven't lived there for months. I left for Scotland months ago."

The inspector leaned back in his chair and stared at the man opposite him. He wasn't a suspect, he was just a man "helping with inquiries," but he was red-faced and fidgeting anxiously, clearly panicked.

"Is this your first time in a police interview room, sir?"

"Yes. And there's no need for it. I had nothing to do with Cartwright's murder."

"Did you know Sir John Cartwright before he bought your house?"

"Yes, slightly. I got to know him better when we were going through the selling process. He came to look at the property several times."

Nicholls had conducted many, many police interviews and knew instinctively the best approach to take. Suspects such as Harry Cooper were on edge before a question had even been asked. What the inspector had to uncover was whether this discomfort was down to fear or guilt. Usually, it took the right kind of pressure, applied with expert timing, to get to the truth. And thanks to Annabelle, the inspector had an ace up his sleeve.

"Do you smoke, Mr. Cooper?"

"Yes."

"Did you smoke at *Woodlands Manor* when you owned it?"

"Yes. Well, my wife never liked me smoking, so I would smoke in the grounds."

"So you knew the grounds well."

"Of course. They were mine for years."

"And your wife, she didn't like you smoking or she didn't like you smoking in the house?"

"Both."

"Would you say then, that you hid your habit from her?"

"I did my best, yes."

"So you would know where you could and couldn't be seen. Where the secret places were. Where there were spots you could smoke to your heart's content without being disturbed?"

"Well, yes."

"And you say you haven't been to the house since Sir John Cartwright moved in?"

"Well, no. I never said that. I've visited him."

"At *Woodlands Manor*?"

"Yes."

"When?"

"I'm not sure exactly."

Nicholls looked at him skeptically. "No matter, we can check. And you smoked while you were there?"

"Yes, I did."

"Inside the property?"

"No. Outside, like I did when I owned the house. When

he moved to Cornwall, John turned over a new leaf—healthy living and all that. It was one of the main reasons for moving. To get away from his old influences."

"Why the change?"

"I don't know exactly. Just the passage of time, probably. He was getting older. And he had a much younger girl-friend. He probably wanted to stick around as long as possible. He was very into health and fitness as you would expect."

The inspector paused for a second. "Why would I expect that?" he said.

"Because of his plans."

CHAPTER TWENTY-ONE

"HE WAS GOING to turn the property into a health spa. He didn't buy it on his own. He gathered investors and formed a syndicate. The investors purchased shares to buy the house and pay for its conversion. He asked me if I was interested, but I wanted to take my money out of the place and retire."

"Do you know how to use a crossbow, Mr Cooper?"

Harry Cooper sat up straight in his chair. He thrust out his chin. "I most certainly do not."

"So if I go to your home in Scotland I won't find a crossbow or other crossbow paraphernalia? I won't speak to anyone who spent time with you shooting one?"

"No."

Inspector Nicholls leaned further back in his chair and looked at Mr. Cooper as he considered the information he had shared with him. A few hours ago, the SOCO team had discovered Cooper's DNA on the cigarette Annabelle had found in the trees. It seemed like a lock— Cooper was their man. He knew the layout of the grounds, places he couldn't be seen. He had been standing at precisely the spot from where the arrow was fired. He knew Sir John well enough to know his movements, to plan an attack. And he was evasive about the date of his recent visit.

And yet, something wasn't right with this sweating, terrified person on the other side of the interview table. The inspector hadn't told Cooper about the DNA. Nicholls had given him the perfect opportunity to cover his tracks with a false story. But Harry hadn't taken it. He had admitted to being at the property and smoking there. He didn't know how to shoot a crossbow. He seemed to have sold the property fairly and retired to Scotland to live quietly. What was his motive for killing John Cartwright?

There was a knock and the door to the interview room opened. "Inspector," said a voice. Nicholls turned to look into the face of a young constable. "Phone call for you, sir. It's urgent."

"More important than an interview?"

"It's a Reverend Annabelle Dixon of Upton St. Mary," the officer replied.

"Okay," the inspector said, stopping the tape recorder and getting up out of his chair. Outside the room, he took the phone. "Reverend?"

"Hello, Inspector Nicholls," came Annabelle's distinctly chirpy voice.

"I'm glad you called. I was just interviewing the man whose cigarette butt you found."

"Oh, do you think he did it?"

"I don't know. I get the impression the situation is more complicated than it seems. He was the owner of *Woodlands Manor* before Sir John Cartwright bought it from him."

"Harry Cooper?"

"Yes, do you know him?"

"Slightly, just to say hello to. We didn't see him much. Just at the pub or in a shop or two. Certainly not at church."

"I've learned that Sir John bought the house as part of a syndicate that was going to turn it into a health spa. Have you heard anything like that?"

"Actually, I have, Inspector. I had two women, French tourists they said they were, in my living room, drinking tea and asking about the dead man. They said something about an investment and I heard them mention a name. I think it was that of the woman who was at the house on the day of the murder. That's why I'm calling."

"What was the name?"

"Poppy Franklin. I've learned that she was living with Sir John in London, and she may have come with him to Upton St. Mary."

"And you think that was the blond woman you saw? At the manor house?"

"Most likely."

"Hold on, Reverend," the inspector said. He turned to the PC next to him and asked him to run a check. There was a pause while he waited for the results. "So we have a record for that name. She's on parole," Nicholls said into the phone as he scanned the computer screen. "She was jailed a few years ago for theft, let off with a light sentence because she claimed her then-boyfriend had coerced her into it. Hmm... Seems John Cartwright employed her when she left prison."

"Oh, my!"

"I'll put a call out. We'll find her as soon as we can. This is fantastic information, Reverend. You have come to the rescue."

"Oh, think nothing of it. I only want to help," Annabelle said.

"I owe you one, Reverend."

"Well, there is one thing, Inspector."

"What is it?"

"I'd like to take another look inside *Woodlands Manor*. I know it's a crime scene, but I'd only need a few minutes. I have a theory..."

"Of course, it's just gathering dust now. Constable Raven has the key."

"Oh, that's ever so kind of you, Inspector. Thank you! I'll get right over there."

CHAPTER TWENTY-TWO

ANNABELLE DRUMMED HER fingers on the kitchen table. Gazing out of the window at the church, she waited for Constable Jim Raven's police car to pull up alongside her cottage. She was anxious to be on her way to *Woodlands Manor* with the keys Jim had promised to drop off.

With Philippa keeping a close eye on the two "French tourists" and Inspector Nicholls on the hunt for the young woman from the manor, Annabelle was left to wonder the identity of the person who had let out the scream she had heard shortly before discovering John Cartwright's body. Her mind had thought of and ruled out plenty of possibilities. She had the idea that it could have been an animal but she had dismissed it—Annabelle knew what an animal sounded like. Then she thought it might have been some kind of "death groan," but when she'd mentioned it to Harper, the pathologist said it wasn't possible. Annabelle was stumped. She was so wrapped up in her thoughts that when Jim's patrol car rolled into her driveway, she was polite but refused to chat. She was eager to set off.

As soon as she got to the house, Annabelle slowly made her way up the stairs to the master bedroom. She looked around her, focusing on every detail of the impressive rooms as she looked for anything that might strike her as a clue. If she were less distracted, she might have been frightened. Entering a large, empty house, the scene of a murder just a few days ago, was something for only the very brave or the very determined. In Annabelle's case, her curiosity gave her plenty of courage and grit.

The master bedroom seemed different to her now. Without a dead body on the floor, the room felt lighter, more spacious. After looking around for anything that might have made the screaming sound—an unseen speaker or a discreet TV, maybe—Annabelle decided to investigate the other rooms on the floor.

As she wandered around, Annabelle was taken aback by how beautiful the house was. There were roughly a dozen rooms of all shapes and sizes shooting off from the landing. There were elaborate, luxurious parlors filled with antiques, bedrooms with sumptuous, silk-clad four-poster beds, and tastefully arranged bathrooms with wonderfully preserved original fittings. Annabelle expressed her appreciation by cooing at the sights but didn't notice anything that might have explained the scream. She went back into the master bedroom to stand in the precise spot where she had found Sir John Cartwright's body.

"Right. Let's see. Let's assume the screamer saw the body, screamed, then disappeared before I got here. How would they have done that so quickly?" Annabelle mumbled to herself.

The first possibility was, of course, through the window. Annabelle opened it and looked down at the ground. She immediately gave up on the idea. Not only was the drop legbreakingly long, but there were beds full of shrubs and flowers beneath the window. Even if the screamer had made their way down the wall, they would have left noticeable signs among the plants below.

The other possibility was that the screamer had got out via the bedroom door. But it had been locked and Annabelle doubted there was enough time between the scream and her reaching the room for the person to leave, lock it, and clear the landing. Annabelle studied the lock closely. It was old and well-worn. She remembered how it had given way when she had applied pressure. Stranger still, she discovered that when the door was slammed shut, it would lock itself—such was the weakness in the ancient mechanism. Perhaps it locked by accident in that case? Annabelle shook her head. If the screamer had slammed the door, she would have heard it. Even in her heightened state of fear and excitement, she wouldn't have missed the sound of a slamming door as she rushed up the stairs. Sound traveled very well in the large house.

Annabelle felt frustrated and deflated. Perhaps she would never figure it out. Then she noticed the bathroom. The door was slightly ajar.

Annabelle pushed the door expecting to find something impressive and yet was still stunned by what she saw. The master bathroom was huge. Larger than her living room! She stepped onto the marble-tiled floor, marveling at its extravagance. Along one wall, there were two vast sinks each with a framed mirror set into the wall above them. In one corner, there was a shower stall encased in glass. Annabelle thought it big enough for ten people while in the center of the room, lit by dappled light that poured in through the frosted window, there was a porcelain and cast-iron bath set on four elaborately engraved feet.

Once Annabelle had regained her breath, she scanned the walls and discovered exactly what she had hoped to see. Another door. She marched over to it, cast one last longing look at the opulent bathroom and opened the small, plain wooden door. She went through it like she was passing into another world. And in a way she was because Annabelle found herself in a slim, barren passage, far more rough and dirty than any other part of the house she had been in. Further along, she reached some stairs.

"A servant's passage," Annabelle murmured. "This must have been how they moved things around without being seen. "

Annabelle imagined how many people must have scurried up and down this bare-walled network of steps and passages. They would have been loaded with buckets of hot water for the bath, food for breakfast in bed, or coal for the fireplaces. She explored it carefully, opening doors that poked into various rooms of the house, many of which she hadn't noticed when exploring from the other side. Eventually, Annabelle found herself going down rugged stone steps that seemed to go on and on. Sure enough, the blank white-washed walls of the house's secret passage gave way to the rough, textured stone of a vast coal cellar. There was barely any light, but Annabelle plowed on through the thick, dusty air and long-forgotten cobwebs. Ahead of her, something glowed, and she let it guide her out of the coal cellar and down a long tunnel where wooden rafters held up the stone over her head. Eventually, she emerged through the open entrance to find herself all the way out in the woods!

"This must be where coal and firewood deliveries were made," she said. "I bet there's a road nearby. The perfect getaway for a murderer." She breathed in the cool, clean air, and was struck by a strangely familiar smell. She tried to identify what it was but couldn't place it. She looked around. It was a smell she knew well, of something she liked. It reminded her of her kitchen. Of tea. Of... cupcakes! Annabelle looked down at the ground and saw, barely a few yards away, a stash of stale, nibbled-upon cupcakes. They looked familiar. Annabelle picked one up and sniffed. There was no mistake. They were Philippa's.

"Surely not!" Annabelle prodded at the pile. "And these at the bottom must have been made weeks ago! What has Philippa got to do with this?"

CHAPTER TWENTY-THREE

ANNABELLE SLEPT UNEASILY and woke up in a huff. She washed, dressed, and made herself a small breakfast. Pensively, she ate it at the kitchen table, muttering to herself. Biscuit kept her distance. Much had happened. The case was progressing. However, the one element that bothered Annabelle the most was still a complete mystery. Who was the screamer?

She suspected the inspector didn't believe she had heard a scream, thinking instead that Annabelle had been caught up in the moment. It was understandable—Sir John *had* been murdered over an hour prior, and the arrow's trajectory placed the killer *outside* the building—but it was also frustrating. Annabelle *knew* what she heard.

She glanced at the clock and realized that she had been lost in her breakfast reverie for a little over an hour. She tidied her plates and decided to get out of the house. Her preoccupation with the case had left her with many parish visits to make, and she was determined not to delay them any longer. Unfortunately for her plans, however, the phone rang just as she was about to leave the house.

"Hello, Annabelle speaking."

"Hello, Reverend. We've found Poppy Franklin." It was the inspector. "We interviewed her early this morning."

"Good! What did she say? Did she say why she ran?"

"She said she didn't want to be accused of Sir John Cartwright's murder. Says she caught a glimpse of the dead body, and just ran for it, scared for her life."

"It's possible..."

"Possible but unlikely. Turns out she knows how to use a crossbow."

"Inspector!" Annabelle said. "I didn't mean that. I meant it's likely she was frightened and panicked. You don't really think she committed the murder, do you?"

"Why not? She had the opportunity. Motive, if she stands to inherit. She knew Sir John very well. Claims that she was just his assistant, but I doubt that. We're continuing our investigation into her and Sir John's dealings. And most importantly, she knows how to fire a crossbow. We haven't found the murder weapon yet but we're on it!"

Annabelle thought for a second, recalling the sweet young face of the blond woman at the door. She knew she shouldn't judge a book by its cover, but Annabelle trusted her instincts when it came to people. Poppy Franklin's innocence seemed as clear as day to her. "I just don't believe it, Inspector."

"Look, Annabelle, she confirmed that Sir John Cartwright was planning to convert the house into a health spa, even mentioned some of the other investors by name—"

"What were their names?" interrupted Annabelle. "Who were they?"

"Oh... ah... let me see... A Sophie Fortescue-Brimwill and Gabriella Fabberini. Apparently, they put quite a lot of money into the syndicate. Why do you ask?"

"I think you'll find that they were the women who were in my living room the other day," Annabelle said. "The 'French tourists.'"

"They were the people who gave you Poppy's name?"

Annabelle thought back to listening to the two women through the door. "Not exactly, but they are staying at a bed-and-breakfast in the village. Philippa's been monitoring them."

"Okay, we'll speak to them. We'll be holding the Franklin woman for twenty-four hours. If we get nothing more, we'll have to let her go, but I think we'll have enough to make a case."

"You may have enough to make a case, Inspector, but will it be the correct one?" There was a long pause. "Are you alright, Reverend?" Nicholls said eventually.

"Yes, yes," replied Annabelle. "Bye, Inspector."

"Bye, Reverend, take care. Stop worrying about the case, it's up to us to take it from here."

Annabelle replaced the handset and held her hand there for a long time, biting her lip. She left the house and got into her car, driving out of the carpark and toward the center of the village. She was not happy. It was she who had given Poppy Franklin's name to the police. When the whole, horrid affair had occurred, Annabelle would have been satisfied offering whatever help she could. Now, she felt responsible for its successful—and proper —conclusion.

Something within Annabelle stirred. Something wasn't quite right. In fact, it felt entirely *wrong*. In a rare, sudden example of reckless driving, Annabelle spun her Mini in a sharp U-turn—nearly knocking Mr. Hawthorne off his bike. His pipe fell out of his pocket.

"Sorry, Mr. Hawthorne!" Annabelle shouted out of the

window, as he watched her, slack-jawed, take the road to Truro.

CHAPTER TWENTY-FOUR

ANNABELLE MARCHED INTO Truro police station with all the determination of someone who had a job to do and who was jolly well going to do it.

"Good morning, Reverend!" the desk officer said, cheerfully.

"Hello, Officer. I'm here to see Inspector Nicholls."

"Right you are. Follow me."

When Inspector Nicholls saw Annabelle approach his office, he rubbed his eyes and took another sip of coffee, believing the late nights and stress of a perplexing murder case must be causing him to hallucinate.

"Hello, Inspector," Annabelle said confirming she was not, in fact, a mirage.

"Reverend, is something the matter? We only just spoke an hour ago."

"Yes, Inspector. I insist on speaking to Poppy Franklin."

Nicholls studied Annabelle's face for a sign that this was a joke. "Are you serious? With all due respect, Reverend, I can't allow just anyone to speak to her."

"I understand that, Inspector, but I believe she is innocent. And I'd like the opportunity to prove it."

"What makes you think she's innocent?"

"Faith, Inspector. Intuition."

The inspector sighed.

"I'm going to need more than that, Reverend. However much I'd like to use faith and intuition in my police work, it doesn't operate like that."

"Inspector," Annabelle said, putting some steel into her voice. She leaned over and placed a firm hand on his desk, fixing Nicholls with a stare. "I have helped you at every stage of this investigation. It isn't arrogant of me to say that I have provided you with some crucial pieces of evidence. I'm asking you to consider my trustworthiness, diligence, and abilities before you dismiss my request."

The inspector sighed again and looked over at the constable who was standing behind Annabelle. The constable raised his eyebrows.

"I do appreciate everything you've done, Reverend, But I've interviewed her already," Nicholls said. "I don't want to put more pressure on her unnecessarily. She's already shaken up. I don't see what you could ask that would help."

"You said she knew how to use a crossbow."

"Yes, she admitted it."

"Did you ask her *where* she learned how to use a crossbow? Or who taught her?"

The inspector rubbed a hand across his stubble. He stood up. "Okay, I'll give you five minutes," he said. He turned to the constable who was paying close attention. "And don't you tell anyone I did this."

Inspector Nicholls took Annabelle to a cell and opened the door. Annabelle stepped inside.

Poppy Franklin looked vastly different from the perky,

pleasant woman who had answered the door to Annabelle a couple of weeks earlier. She sat on the concrete bed, hunched over, her arms wrapped around her sides in a hug. Brown mascara marked her pale cheeks in vertical streaks. "Reverend?" she whispered, her puffy red eyes squinting as if she couldn't believe what she saw.

"Poppy? Oh dear," Annabelle said, sitting beside the woman and putting an arm around her.

Poppy allowed Annabelle to hold her. She relaxed. Annabelle was warm and soft. She smelled of lavender. The young woman struggled not to burst into tears again. "Why...? What are you doing here?" Poppy pulled away from Annabelle to look up into her sympathetic face.

"I'm here to help you. But I need you to answer something for me."

"What? Anything, if you can get me out of here."

"Inspector Nicholls said you told him you knew how to use a crossbow."

The woman sat up. She looked down at her lap, her hair falling across her face so that Annabelle couldn't see her properly. "Yes, that's right."

"Poppy, I need you to tell me who taught you."

Poppy looked away from Annabelle as if the question had slapped her across the face. "I can't."

"Poppy..."

"No. I'm sorry."

"Poppy, it's probable they won't be able to accuse you of murder but if you don't help, they will almost certainly charge you with being an accessory. You're the only person who's admitted to knowing how to use a crossbow. You were in the house when the murder occurred. You ran from the scene of the crime. Whomever you're protecting, you'll pay a big price for doing so."

"No," Poppy stuttered, through sobs.

Annabelle pulled a pack of tissues from her pocket and handed them to the shuddering woman. "You're innocent, Poppy, I know you are. You did nothing wrong. That's why this is difficult for you. You're trapped somehow. Tell me the truth, and set things right."

Poppy looked up from the scrunched-up tissues she held and into Annabelle's compassionate eyes.

"Go on," Annabelle urged.

Poppy sighed. Her shoulders dropped two inches. "William...Will," Poppy said suddenly. "Will Conran. He's a friend of mine—my ex-boyfriend. He taught me. We've known each other since we were kids."

Annabelle rubbed Poppy's back. She could feel the relief flooding through the younger woman's slim body as if purging a poison she had held in for a very long time.

"He's always been an archer. He moved on to crossbows in his late teens. Goes hunting regularly. Sometimes he'd go on several trips a week."

"You think Will might have shot Sir John?"

"I don't know for sure, but I think so."

"Why?"

Poppy's sobs grew a little louder, and it took a while for Annabelle to calm her down. Eventually, Poppy turned to Annabelle and gathering all the strength she had, she said, "Because he thinks I left him for Sir John."

CHAPTER TWENTY-FIVE

THE NEXT FEW hours were a flurry of activity and noise. Once Annabelle had given the inspector the name, Will Conran, he sprang into action. With the information sent to police stations across the nation, it took barely an hour before they tracked Conran to Reading, a town south of London. Reading police brought him into custody and so it became a matter of Inspector Nicholls driving there to question him. He immediately threw on his trench coat and made for the police station exit.

"You coming, Reverend?" he asked.

Annabelle had been milling around the station, caught up in the excitement. But now she found herself utterly befuddled. "Me?"

"Do you see any other vicars around here?"

"You want *me* to come with you to Reading to interrogate the suspect?"

"Why not? As you said, each time we've made a breakthrough, you're involved. Either you're very good at this or extremely lucky. Either way, I'd rather have you with me than not."

Annabelle beamed. "Of course, Inspector. Lead the way."

As the convoy of police cars set off into the early evening with a flurry of squealing sirens and flashing lights, Annabelle found herself giddy with excitement. This was certainly a change of pace from the summer fête. She couldn't wait to tell Philippa!

They arrived as it was getting dark. The larger, busier atmosphere of the Reading station intimidated Annabelle, she felt a little over her head. But she said a short prayer and prepared herself to accomplish what she had set out to do since the beginning—discover the truth.

Inspector Nicholls exchanged a few words with the Reading duty officer. Nicholls pointed at Annabelle and she saw them look at her. She looked at the ground and missed the inspector raise a placating hand to the duty officer as he spoke. Nicholls must have been persuasive because soon Annabelle was accompanying him to the interview room where Will Conran was being held.

When she walked into the room, Annabelle's eyes widened a fraction before she wrestled her face into a neutral expression. In front of her was the young man who had picked up her bread rolls outside the bakery on the day of the murder. Conran was in his mid-twenties and with his chiseled jawline and sparkling blue eyes, Annabelle couldn't help but think what an attractive couple he and Poppy must have made.

"Why are you here?" snarled Will. He wasn't at all the helpful person he'd been outside the bakery.

"New kind of justice system," Nicholls said. He pulled

out a chair for Annabelle. "If you're guilty, she'll send your soul straight to hell." He pressed the button to start the interview tape and stated the date, time, and their names.

"Guilty of what?" Will barked.

"You know what," the inspector growled back. He, too, had lost his charm.

"I don't know what you're talking about."

The inspector leaned over to Annabelle and whispered in her ear. "This might take some time."

Annabelle looked at the inspector, then back at Conran. She didn't have time. She had to be back in Upton St. Mary for the Women's Institute fundraising meeting tomorrow. The last one had broken up in uproar when someone suggested holding a paid life drawing class, and seventy-year-old Mrs. Bellichamp had offered to be the model.

"Poppy is in utter pieces!" Annabelle exclaimed loudly, taking both men by surprise. "She's in a terrible state! And she's in that state because of you!" The inspector put his hand on Annabelle's arm to calm her down, but her eyes locked with Conran's.

"Poppy's just a friend..." the man murmured. He slouched in his seat, looking like a sullen teenager.

"She's more than a friend," Annabelle replied, sharply.

"Not for a long time," came Will's reply. His voice shook. The inspector removed his hand from Annabelle's arm.

"So you don't care about her?" Annabelle said.

"I... I care about her as much as she cares about me. So no, I don't."

"If she didn't care about you," Annabelle continued, lowering her voice to deliver the blow, "then why would she protect you?"

Conran looked up. "She... protected me? From what?"

"It took her this long to give us your name in connection with the murder of John Cartwright," Nicholls said. "She was uncooperative for ages."

Will shook his head. "I didn't do anything. There's nothing to protect me from."

CHAPTER TWENTY-SIX

T HE THREE OF them sat in silence.

"Well," Annabelle said, "if you didn't do anything, then Poppy is off to jail for a very long time."

Will's eyes widened. Annabelle stood up slowly. The inspector ended the interview, turned off the tape, and followed suit.

"Wait!" Will said. Annabelle and the inspector froze.

"You... You can't arrest Poppy for this. You know she wouldn't hurt a fly."

"We can, and we will," the inspector replied. "She knows how to use a crossbow. She was at the scene of the crime. And she was close enough to John Cartwright to benefit from his death. Means, motive, opportunity. That'll go a lot further in court than you appearing as a character witness for her."

Will looked between the pair opposite him, his eyes darting about before he slumped over the table, his head in his hands. "Okay," he mumbled. He dragged his hands down his face leaving pink and white marks.

"What was that?" the inspector asked. "I didn't hear you."

Will raised his head and spoke more clearly. "Okay, I'll talk."

Annabelle and the inspector took their seats again. The inspector turned the tape back on. He gestured for Will to start speaking.

"Me and Poppy grew up together. She was my childhood sweetheart. We were together all through our teenage years. I loved her more than anything, but I made a lot of mistakes. Took her for granted. I wasn't as nice to her as I should have been."

"You made her steal for you," the inspector said.

"Yeah, don't get me wrong though. Poppy was no angel. She liked nice things, expensive things. Clothes, make-up, you know how women are. I got into shoplifting, and she started doing it too. It's easier to get away with when you look as innocent as she does.

"But then we got nicked. We'd already been caught a few times, but this time, it was big. We were breaking into a store. I ended up doing time. Four years. Poppy got one because her lawyer said I forced her to do it."

"And that made you bitter?" the inspector prodded, again.

Will answered with an empty laugh. "No, that's not what made me bitter," he said, his eyes alive with anger before the fire faded and was replaced with regret. "I would've done two extra years if it meant Poppy did none, but I expected her to wait for me. To support me. To appreciate what I had done for her all through our time together. Instead..." Will looked at the wall, unseeing, lost in his memories.

"She found John Cartwright," Annabelle said, as softly as she could. "Or John Cartwright found her."

Will slammed his fist against the table. "Can you believe it?! An old pervert more than twice her age! She was only meant to work for him a bit, do some stupid maid stuff in one of his fancy houses in the city. I knew he was after her from the start, but she wouldn't listen. The next thing I know, she's all, 'I can't live this life anymore, visiting you in jail, scratching a living. We both need a fresh start.'"

"That's when she came to Upton St. Mary?" asked the inspector.

"Yeah."

"And you followed her?" Annabelle said.

"Yeah," Will said, quietly. "When I got out of prison, I went straight down there."

"Okay," the inspector said, patiently. "Then what?"

"I wanted to learn a bit about what they were doing there. I hung around and stuff, in the pubs and that. Listened in to people's conversations. And did they have something to say about Cartwright? Eventually, I found out that he'd bought the house from some guy who'd moved up to Scotland but who was visiting."

"Harry Cooper."

"Yeah, that was him. I got him drunk in the pub one night. We got talking. He obviously knew the property. He told me about a secret entrance to the house, the coal cellar shaft that came out in the woods. He said you could see right into Cartwright's bedroom from one spot. "

"The spot you killed him from," Nicholls said.

Will glared at the inspector. "I already told you. I didn't kill anyone."

CHAPTER TWENTY-SEVEN

ANNABELLE AND THE inspector exchanged looks. "If you didn't kill him, then who did? Poppy's the only person on our list," the inspector said.

"I'm not saying anything," Will sneered.

"That's the same thing."

Will broke into a pained smile. "You wouldn't pin this on Poppy. You know she's innocent."

The inspector smiled back. Hardball was the inspector's favorite game. "You've already been to prison, Mr. Conran," Nicholls said. "You know how many unfortunate people there are in there. People who were in the wrong place at the wrong time. Sir John was a knight of the realm, so I'm not putting his death in the 'unsolved' section —*somebody* has to go down for his murder."

"But not Poppy..."

"Look," the inspector said, leaning forward. His eyes glittered. "I've been on this case for weeks now. Everyone in this room knows you did it. But if you don't talk, Poppy's the closest thing to you I've got."

Will took deep lungfuls of air. He glanced around the room as if searching for an escape route. He looked like a cornered animal.

"I'm sure it won't come to that," Annabelle said quietly. Will looked at her. Unlike the two snarling men, she was calm, tranquil. "So tell us what did happen. You were in the woods, at *Woodlands Manor*."

"Yeah," Will mumbled, dropping his head, "Harry Cooper told me it was a good spot for hunting, a lot of pheasants and even some rabbits. So that's what I did. I went hunting."

The inspector snorted. "Don't try and tell me you killed him by accident."

"I'm telling you I went hunting. Yeah, I wanted to see the house for myself, maybe catch a glimpse of Poppy, but I was there to hunt."

"So how does that end up with you shooting him?"

"What did you see while you were there, Will?" Annabelle said. "Did you see Poppy? Did she see you?"

Will looked around him once again, breathing through his nose like an angry bull, but when his eyes met those of Annabelle, the fire went out. His eyes dulled, the muscle at his jaw stopped twitching. "I saw him with Poppy. I think she saw me too. They were walking around, talking and laughing, just like we used to. I couldn't believe it.... Couldn't believe how he acted like she was his. It made me furious. It still does."

"So you shot him?" Annabelle gently probed.

"I just sat there, getting madder and madder. I felt like I was going to explode. I had never hated anyone so much as I hated him at that moment. Then he opened the windows and just sat there with that smug look on his face. His eyes weren't even open. I had the crossbow in my hand and the next second, my arrow was gone. I don't even remember loading it."

Will swallowed hard before continuing. "I shot him, and then I just froze, staring at the window. He'd disappeared but hadn't made a sound. Then I started running. I didn't know if I had killed him or even hit him, but I just had to get away." Neither Annabelle nor the inspector moved. "But then I stopped. I realized I needed to find out what I'd done. I needed to see him with my own eyes. I knew Poppy would be in the house, but I just wanted to see *him*." Will stopped.

"Go on," Annabelle said softly.

"I found the cellar entrance just where Harry Cooper had told me and ran into it and through the house. I don't know how, but I ended up in a bathroom, a big, fancy bathroom."

"I heard a car on the gravel outside. I wasn't sure what to do, so I waited. I waited a long time. I heard the car drive away but still, I stayed where I was. I felt like I was going insane. I was trying to calm myself down, but I had to know if I'd killed him. And then, just as I was about to look for the old man, the car came back! So I just went for it. Through the bathroom door and into the bedroom. The old man was spread out on the floor with an arrow through his heart, dead as the crows I used to shoot when I was a kid. When I saw his body, I was so angry, so pumped-up, so crazed, I yelled my head off. Then I heard loud footsteps and I rushed back the way I came, through the coal cellar, through the woods, and to the road. I didn't stop until I was back in Reading."

Will looked at the inspector who calmly stared back at him. The young man looked at Annabelle. Her eyes were big, her lashes slowly fluttering down and up. Will sat back in his chair and put his hands on his head. He looked up at the ceiling. He seemed exhausted by his confession. It was over, and the tension in the room dissipated, leaving nothing but regret and sorrow.

Nicholls rose to his feet and tapped Annabelle on the shoulder to do the same. "You'll be going to jail for a very long time, Mr. Conran," he said. "Murder, manslaughter if you're lucky."

"I know," Will mumbled. "But at least Poppy will be free."

"I think you were wrong, you know," Annabelle said. "I really think she did want a different life. And her relationship with Cartwright was purely professional. He had turned his life around, lived healthily and honorably. I believe he was nothing more than her employer and her friend, her platonic friend."

"Maybe," Will said. "But it's too late now."

The inspector guided Annabelle outside. She looked distraught. The inspector placed a gentle hand on her shoulder.

"What an awful tale!" Annabelle said.

The inspector nodded slowly. "Emotions, they can be the devil. Now he'll spend years in jail, reflecting on one moment of madness."

CHAPTER TWENTY-EIGHT

A S HER BLUE Mini rolled into her parking spot at the church, Annabelle noticed a light on in her cottage. It could only mean that Philippa was there.

"Hello, Annabelle," Philippa said, as she wiped her hands on her apron. "I was just washing the church bowls. I'll be done in a jiffy."

"Actually, Philippa," Annabelle said. "I'd like to speak to you."

"Oh?" Philippa said. Annabelle was using a tone she reserved for bad news. "I see."

Annabelle took off her coat and hung it up while Philippa untied her apron. They took seats around the kitchen table, facing each other.

"It's time, isn't it, Annabelle?" Philippa said.

"I'm afraid it is," Annabelle replied.

"I've been meaning to bring this up for a long time. I just didn't want to cause a scene," Philippa said.

"I understand, Philippa. It's difficult for me too."

"I didn't want to cause you any problems, Reverend."

"Philippa!" Annabelle gasped. "It's you I'm worried about!"

"That's kind of you."

"Well? What's going on?"

"You tell me." Philippa sighed. She shifted in her seat. "I know about the cakes."

"You know how they got there?"

"I don't know where they are. But I know what happened to them."

"Wait a moment," Annabelle said. "You don't know where they are?"

"Well, I imagine you ate them, Annabelle."

"Philippa! Why would I eat old cupcakes that have been left outside in the rain?"

"Why would you leave them outside in the rain? Oh, Annabelle, you don't even know when you're doing it!"

Annabelle found herself so confused she didn't know what to say. "What are you talking about, Philippa?"

"About the cupcakes, Annabelle!"

"What about them?"

"You steal them!"

Annabelle slumped back in her chair. She had never been accused of theft in her life and certainly not in as strange a manner as this. "Why on earth would I steal cupcakes, Philippa?"

"For the thrill of it. The excitement of the chase. The feeling of getting away with it. It's that kleptomania I told you about! Oh, I know it's not your fault, Annabelle. You can't help it. I see you eat one or two, but then three are gone! You probably stash it in your pocket when I'm not looking. Maybe you feel guilty about eating so many. I don't know, I'm just glad it's out in the open!"

Annabelle couldn't help but smile. Philippa's accusation was absurd, but it also meant that she had nothing to do with what had happened at *Woodlands Manor*. "I can assure you, Philippa, I do not steal cupcakes."

Philippa sighed deeply again. "If not you, then who?"

With the perfect timing, Biscuit squeezed through the cat door and sashayed her way toward her bowl. The two women watched her like she was a model on a catwalk. Biscuit ignored them and began lapping up water, flicking it into her mouth with her tongue.

"I believe we won't need to look for a suspect. The suspect just found us," Annabelle said.

"Biscuit?" Philippa said, incredulous. "That's impossible!"

Annabelle wagged her finger. "Actually, it makes perfect sense. I found her out in the woods a few days ago, right where I found the stash of cupcakes. You said yourself that she had stopped eating, and whenever you bring those cupcakes out, Biscuit seems to make a timely entrance."

"That's incredible!"

"Not really, she's a cat with strange tastes, but then we already knew that. What's incredible is the fact that this is the second mystery I've solved today!"

EPILOGUE

I F THE GROUNDS of *Woodlands Manor* were beautiful before, those of the newly-refurbished *Woodlands Manor Resort & Spa* were spectacular. Annabelle and Philippa gasped with wonder as the Mini made its way up the driveway in a procession of cars.

"They've worked wonders!" Philippa said, pointing at the grass tennis courts to one side.

"Oh look! A pool!" Annabelle exclaimed.

It had been six months since the tragic events at *Woodlands Manor*, yet no signs of those dark circumstances were apparent in this magnificent reinvention. Annabelle slowed the car to a halt just in front of the entrance.

"Oh!" she exclaimed when her driver-side door was opened.

"Ma'am," said the red-suited valet.

Philippa and Annabelle exchanged smiles before clambering out of the car. The valet took Annabelle's keys and gestured to a lawn at the side of the house.

"If you'll just follow the path, ma'am, you'll find the other guests."

"Thank you," Annabelle said, slightly embarrassed. She wasn't used to such deferential treatment.

"I could get used to this," Philippa said.

At the back of the house, lines of buffet tables laden with food were arranged inside a large marquee, a prudent idea for even the sunniest of days thanks to the unpredictability of the British weather. Around the tables, a large crowd of Upton St. Mary villagers unaccustomed to such extravagance stood apart from well-heeled spa patrons, moneyed people from London, and press. The two groups eyed each other carefully in something of a standoff.

As Annabelle and Philippa walked toward the marquee, two women emerged from it with open arms.

"The guests of honor!" Sophie said.

"How wonderful to see you!" Gabriella added.

Annabelle and Philippa prepared to shake hands but were enthusiastically grasped in big hugs. "It is wonderful of you to invite the whole village to the opening. We're excited to see what you've done," Annabelle said.

"And you've brought work to the area," Philippa added. She looked at Annabelle and beamed. Annabelle had gone in to bat for the village and persuaded Sophie and Gabriella to employ villagers as staff, produce suppliers, and gardeners. Philippa's brother had fixed the house's ancient plumbing while others had decorated rooms, installed kitchens, and renovated the historical features of the house.

"Oh, but of course! The villagers are the reason we decided to take on this project," Gabriella said. "After we were left in the lurch rather, after Sir John Cartwright's death, it would have been so easy to abandon our project, but it was their skills and willingness to work hard that persuaded us to roll up our sleeves and get on with it."

"That and Gabriella having grown rather fond of the organic produce," Sophie said, gently patting Gabriella's slightly rounded stomach.

"Speaking of which, I insist you try these chia seed and coconut macaroons," Gabriella said. She led Annabelle and Philippa to one of the buffet tables.

"I've never heard of chia seeds," Philippa said.

"They are *huge* in California, darling," insisted Gabriella. "The health benefits are marvelous."

Annabelle and Philippa took small bites. "Oh. They're very... interesting," Annabelle said, munching purposefully.

"And do try this chamomile tea," Sophie urged. She poured them cups of hot pale yellow liquid.

Philippa and Annabelle sniffed at the tea, and sipped tentatively. Philippa coughed."It's very different from regular tea," she said. She coughed again. Gabriella smiled with pride.

"So, I take it you're here to stay?" Annabelle asked. "Not going to rush off to London and leave this place for someone else to manage?"

"No," Sophie replied. "We are committed. We're going to stay and run this place at least for the next year or two."

"The French tourists have become British residents," joked Gabriella.

"You won't miss the city?" Annabelle asked.

"Well," Sophie began, "some would say that the appeal of fast city life can't be matched. But, as I think you know well enough Annabelle, excitement can crop up in the strangest of places."

The two women excused themselves and Annabelle and Philippa spent a delightful couple of hours touring the spa and chatting to guests before requesting the Mini from the valet and returning home. It was a lovely drive through the lanes, the patchwork of bright green fields dotted with sheep and black and white cows on either side of them under a clear blue sky.

"Cup of tea, Annabelle?" Philippa said as they got back.

"Oh, yes, just what the doctor ordered."

"Chamomile?" Philippa giggled.

"I'll stick with the regular, thanks." Annabelle laughed. "Milk and sugar, please."

Philippa put the pot on the kitchen table and opened the oven. Inside was a tray of fragrant, freshly-baked cupcakes.

"Heavens!" Annabelle exclaimed. "Those look wonderful!"

"They're almond, Annabelle."

"They smell absolutely scrumptious!"

"Thank you. I decided against making baklava."

"Why so?" Annabelle said. She clenched her fists in an attempt to restrain herself. It wouldn't do to grab a cupcake *too* ferociously.

"I think we've had enough drama in Upton St. Mary for a while. We don't need more."

There was a rattle and Biscuit appeared through the cat door. "Meow." The ginger cat sat in her favorite position by the door.

"Don't worry, Annabelle," Philippa said. "I'm keeping my eye on that cat. She won't be stealing any more of these cupcakes. She's on a strict diet of chicken bits and fish now. She could do with losing a few pounds too."

"Philippa!" Annabelle said. "To what are you inferring?"

"Well, Annabelle, you know, the inspector..."

"Our relationship is strictly professional," Annabelle countered, restraining herself no longer. She reached out and picked up a cupcake. Holding Philippa's gaze, she took a big bite and munched on the soft, feathery sponge. One might almost say she did so defiantly.

"Yes, Annabelle, sorry," Philippa said. "Though I daresay you impressed him—in a professional capacity, of course."

Annabelle focused on sipping her tea and eating her cupcake. The two women were silent for a few moments, enjoying the peace and quiet of a country afternoon that was broken only by the occasional chirping of a bird outside.

Annabelle swallowed the last of her cake and reached for another, before pausing halfway. She considered for a moment, before catching Philippa's eye.

"Oh, go on, Annabelle. You deserve it," Philippa said with a smile.

Thank you for reading *Murder at the Mansion*! I hope you love Annabelle as much as I do. Her story continues in *Body in the Woods*.

A dark discovery. Buried bones. A sweet confection of lost love and murder...

When a young boy running through the woods unearths a buried human bone, a cold case is soon re-opened. And Reverend Annabelle Dixon, with her insatiable appetite for mystery and crime, simply can't leave it alone.

On a sugar high, Annabelle gets herself into a new series of scrapes. A newcomer to the village has his heart set on love. The antagonism with her crush, Inspector Nicholls grows. And church secretary Philippa supplies Annabelle with gossip, cake, and her own little puzzle that gets the vicar a-thinking. What will become of them all? And will Annabelle solve the decades-old mystery? Order Body in the Woods from Amazon to find out! Body in the Woods is FREE in Kindle Unlimited.

To find out about new books, sign up for my newsletter: https://www.alisongolden.com

If you love the Reverend Annabelle series, you'll want to read the *USA Today* bestselling Inspector Graham series featuring a new and unusual detective with a phenomenal memory and a tragic past. The first in the series, *The Case of the Screaming Beauty* is available for purchase from Amazon and FREE in Kindle Unlimited..

And don't miss the Roxy Reinhardt mysteries. Will Roxy triumph after her life falls apart? She's fired from her job, her boyfriend dumps her, she's out of money. So, on a whim, she goes on the trip of a lifetime to New Orleans, There, she gets mixed up in a Mardi Gras murder. *Things were going to be fine. They were, weren't they?* Get the first in the series, Mardi Gras Madness from Amazon. Also FREE in Kindle Unlimited!

If you're looking for something edgy and dangerous, root for Diana Hunter as she seeks justice after a devastating crime destroys her family. Start following her journey in this non-stop series of suspense and action by purchasing Hunted, the prequel to the series.

Hunted is FREE in Kindle Unlimited.

I hugely appreciate your help in spreading the word about *Murder at the Mansion*, including telling a friend. Reviews help readers find books! Please leave a review on your favorite book site.

Turn the page for an excerpt from the next book in the Reverend Annabelle series, *Body in the Woods...*

A Reverend Annabelle Dixon Mystery

BODY IN THE WOODS

Alison Golden

Jamie Vougeot

BODY IN THE WOODS
CHAPTER ONE

IT HAD BEEN a tough week for young Master Douglas "Dougie" Dewar. It had begun with him tearing his school uniform during a particularly ambitious tree-climbing adventure, continued with reprisals about his over-active imagination from his teacher Miss Montgomery, and reached its peak when Aunt Shona discovered he had been trying to rustle sheep by training none other than the church cat, a ginger tabby named Biscuit.

How could they blame him? He had been in Upton St. Mary for only four months since his mother had sent him there from their home in Edinburgh, and he still found the village and the vibrant countryside surrounding it full of possibilities.

He would trek the rolling hills armed only with a trusty stick and an insisted-upon sandwich, imagining himself a brave adventurer on a quest to find a wise, old wizard. He would swing from tree branches like a wilderness warrior, announcing his presence with a signature yell, determined to save all of civilization, reaping world domination as his prize. And he would creep through the dense forest, envisioning it as some deep, exotic jungle on a strange new planet, while encountering delicate, well-camouflaged wildlife that demonstrated all the curiosity and nervousness of timid alien visitors.

For Dougie was not just energetic and rambunctious of body, but of mind as well. When he wasn't scampering through the rolling countryside in search of adventures, he was poring over pages of the most astonishing and outlandish tales he could find, stoking the fires of his imagination before he lived out his fantasies against Cornwall's glorious pastoral background.

Oh yes, it had been a tough week indeed, but it had also been an incredibly fun one.

Now it was Friday, and the glorious feeling of being on the precipice of the weekend's adventures had Dougie running wildly through the forest on his way home from school. After his mishap earlier in the week, Aunt Shona had insisted he change out of his uniform when he got home before embarking on his adventures. It was a small price to pay, thought Dougie, as he darted, jumped, and swerved around the various tree trunks. But he wasn't home yet.

"No more school," he shouted, as he deftly switched his weight from one foot to another to avoid slipping on a tree root. "No more Miss Montgomery!" As he kept on running, he ran through his weekend plans. "I'll meet the boys to play football tomorrow, and then Aunt Shona promised me a trip to the bookstore. Gonna get the next in the 'Reptiloid Hunter' series. Woo-hoo!"

His imagination ran wild with excitement. He ducked his head and pictured himself a spaceship shooting through an asteroid field. He skipped off a bank and fancied himself on a flying carpet. He spread his arms and turned sharply like a fighter jet, his school satchel sailing behind him like a tail.

Just as he was about to bank sharply again and release another barrage of missiles, however, Dougie found himself genuinely floating in mid-air, his feet up behind him. For a split second, he almost believed he was flying.

"Oof!" he grunted as he landed on his chest atop the tough late summer soil.

Dougie bounced back up almost immediately, his youthful exuberance overwhelming the sharp pain in his elbow and the winded sensation in his chest.

"Oh no! I'm going to be grounded for a week!" he cried as he looked down at the dirt and grass firmly embedded into his school uniform. Cautiously, he checked the spot where the stinging sensation was coming from on his elbow.

"Noooooo!" was all Dougie could muster. He had been well-schooled in the art of politeness and not even being alone in the middle of the woods was enough for him to forget his good manners and utter anything ruder – however much the frayed tear on his blazer warranted it.

He spun around, his pained expression turning to one of anger. Whichever tree root was responsible was going to get it. He took a few steps toward the spot at which he tripped and scanned for the offending object.

The thin, bar-like protrusion which jutted out of the ground at a low angle was not like any tree root Dougie had ever seen. In fact, he had never come across anything remotely like it on his treasure hunts across the forest. He knelt and brushed some of the dirt away.

As he uncovered more of the thin, white oddity, Dougie's heart seemed to sink lower, until it turned a somer-sault. He knew what this was. They had studied the human skeleton just last week in class.

Dougie's mouth opened slowly as he stared at the bone, his mind searching for another, less terrifying prospect. Suddenly, he found himself out of all other potential explanations and incredibly afraid. He hopped to his feet and sprinted toward Aunt Shona's cottage – only this time he was trying to stifle his imagination rather than explore it.

"The boy's fine," Shona Alexander assured her sister on the phone, "he's a little scamp. With a boy like him you only need to worry about when he's *not* up to something... Oh, of course he misses you. He asks after you every chance he gets... He's still so distracted by the excitement of a new place... You've got enough to worry about right now with the chemo, Olivia, just let me take care of Dougie for now... Oh, wait, I think I hear him coming in. I'll get him to call you later, okay? Bye, Olivia."

Shona placed the receiver down gently and turned around.

"That was your mot—"

"Aunt Shona!"

Shona and Dougie stared at each other, each bearing an expression of absolute horror.

"Good Lord, Dougie! Look at you!"

"There's a... There's... It's... I don't know why it's there!"

"Is that a rip? Turn around! Turn around, now! Oh dear Lord..."

"No, Aunt Shona... I saw a... It was right there!"

"What was?"

"A... It looked like... There's a... There's a dead body in the woods!"

"Oh, there'll be a dead body in the woods, alright, if you don't explain to me how you made a mess of yourself when I specifically told you not to go running about before coming home to change."

"Really, Aunt Shona! There's a bone sticking out!"

"Sticking out of where?"

"Out of the ground! I tripped over it!"

Shona placed two hands upon her hips and circled Dougie as if inspecting a car she was considering buying. She shook her head as she noticed every stain, assessing how much time it would take to get each one out.

"You really do have quite an imagination. I hope you realize this means you won't be playing soccer this weekend, young man!"

Dougie stamped his foot impertinently and cried out desperately. "I don't care about the football! There's a dead body in the woods!"

Bizarrely, Shona found Dougie's first statement more surprising than the second, and when she saw the earnestness in the boy's face, she realized that he meant both of them sincerely. Dougie certainly attracted more than his fair share of trouble, but if anything, it was his open, impulsive nature that drew him to it, rather than his proclivity to spin tall tales.

"Sit down," Shona commanded the boy, as she pulled out a chair and sat on it. "Tell me exactly what happened."

Inspector Mike Nicholls was in no mood for games and hadn't been for a while. He had grumbled and complained his way through each workday for over two weeks, and yet his fellow officers had grown none the wiser as to the cause.

Nothing out of the ordinary had happened, and the incidents they had dealt with were remarkable only in their consistency and mildness. Even the weather hadn't been so bad. Yet not even a cup of tea could be served to the Detective Inspector without vociferous criticism about its sweetness or lack thereof. He did not hold back expounding on any other grievance he found pertaining to the cup in question, either. The tea might be too hot, too cold, too strong, or the wrong kind of brew entirely. Officers within his vicinity were liable to receive spiked comments about their manner or work ethic, and even those not present would be noted for their absence, the reasons for which were undoubtedly nefarious in the Inspector's newly negative outlook.

So when the call came from Constable Raven that drove the Inspector to leave the city for the countryside immediately, the officers of Truro police station breathed a sigh of relief before drawing straws to decide who would go with him. Constable Colback drew the short one.

After a long trip, during which Inspector Nicholls articulated his grievances on topics as wide-ranging as long car journeys, people wasting police time, the declining standards of police ceremonies, and the road manners of his fellow drivers, he and his bedraggled constable met the local village bobby, Constable Raven, outside Shona Alexander's house.

"Hello Inspector! Long time no see," said Constable Raven, more cheerily than the grave circumstances demanded.

"I have a forensic team on standby, Constable," the Inspector responded curtly. "So I sincerely hope this is not a waste of time."

Picking up on the Inspector's unusually stern tone, Raven stood upright.

"I don't think so, Inspector. Ms. Alexander and Dougie, her young nephew, sound very concerned."

"How old's the boy?" the Inspector asked.

"I believe he's eight, sir," Raven replied.

"Wait a minute, Constable," Nicholls said, a dark cloud passing over his face. "Are you telling me that I've just put all my other duties aside, made a formal request for the forensic team to enter the area, and driven for almost an hour, based on the story that a schoolboy told his aunt? You didn't check the site yourself?"

Constable Raven struggled to disguise his gulp. He was an informal but effective officer, though diligence and rigor had never been his strengths. Under the intense glare of the Inspector, he suddenly wished they were.

"I didn't want to disturb the scene, Inspector. I thought it right that you be here to witness it first."

DI Nicholls winced, opened his mouth to say something, decided against it, and walked up the pathway to Shona Alexander's door, leaving Constables Raven and Colback to exchange sympathetic glances.

"I'm Detective Inspector Nicholls," he said to the blond woman who opened the door, "I believe you are Ms. Shona Alexander and this lad is Dougie Dewar?"

"Yes, thank you for coming, Inspector."

The Inspector crouched, bringing himself to eye-level with the freshly-washed boy who clung to his aunt's trouser leg.

"What did you see out there, boy?"

After a few seconds, Dougie gathered up the courage to speak.

"There was this bone. An arm bone, sticking out of the ground. I tripped on it and got mud and dirt all over me."

"How big?"

Dougie raised his hands and held them about four inches apart. Nicholls looked around to cast another stern glare at Constable Raven.

"Now are you sure it wasn't a twig? A strange stick, or maybe something plastic?"

Dougie shook his head, too intimidated by the Inspector's direct, unyielding approach to speak.

"A lot of animals have bones, you know. Tell me why you think this was a human bone? An arm, you say?"

"I studied the skeleton at school last week. It has a curve like this," Dougie said, proudly tracing his finger along his forearm, "and another bone next to it like this. That's what it looked like."

Nicholls sighed deeply.

"Well, let's get to it then. The young lad can show us the path and tell us about it on the way."

The detective stood up and began walking back down the path, followed by Dougie and his Aunt Shona. As he passed Constable Raven, he glowered once again and said:

"I hope this kid's knowledge of anatomy is better than your knowledge of police procedure, Constable. For all our sakes."

The sky was turning a dark shade of orange as the five figures approached the long shadows of the woods. Though the days still bore the pleasant warmth and brightness of summer, the sharp decrease in temperature as the sun set over the hills indicated that the warm season was about to be chased away. There was a little crunch in the rustle of leaves underfoot, and the fervent greens that rolled away in all directions began to wane into shades less vivid as encroaching hues of brown and yellow made themselves apparent.

Though Dougie was meant to lead them, he shuffled along beside his Aunt Shona, clutching her hand, while Inspector Nicholls strode forward, setting a brisk pace. Constables Raven and Colback brought up the rear, chatting a little and scanning the surroundings purposefully when they thought Nicholls was watching.

DI Nicholls turned to Dougie as they passed through another clump of trees and began to navigate the deepening shade of the dense forest. Dougie, still rather intimidated by the Inspector's intense silence, raised his arm and pointed ahead, a little to one side. Nicholls nodded once and continued onwards determinedly.

"There!" Dougie squealed suddenly. "That's where I fell! So the bone is..."

Everyone watched the boy's finger trace a trajectory in the air until it pointed to a spot on the ground. Dougie stepped back and pressed himself up against Aunt Shona's trouser leg once again.

DI Nicholls almost leaped toward the spot Dougie had indicated, followed closely by the two constables. They gazed at the strange protrusion for a few seconds, musing over its unusual shape.

"Take the woman and the boy to the edge of the forest, Colback. It's a little way over. You can meet the forensic team there if we need them. Constable Raven?"

"Yes sir?"

"Help me dig it out a little – carefully."

"Yes sir."

As Shona walked after Constable Colback, pulling Dougie away and holding his head so that he couldn't look back, Nicholls and Raven pulled away at the dirt from which the bone emerged. After almost ten minutes of clawing at the ground, growing increasingly impatient, they unearthed what was unmistakably a human elbow.

DI Nicholls pulled out his phone.

"Colback? Call in the forensic team, and bring them over. Tell them we've confirmed it."

Within the hour, night had fallen swiftly and Upton St. Mary had become shrouded in darkness. Drivers on the lazily curving country lanes had to depend on their headlights to see, and the quaint cottages and houses were apparent only by the warm glow coming from their windows and visitor lamps. Few people were outside, most choosing to enjoy the comfort and warmth of their homes, but for those who were, the sky was clear enough for moonlight to help them along their way.

Tonight, however, there were vibrant additions supplementing Upton St. Mary's nighttime illuminations. Multiple police cars had parked by the wall of trees at the woods' edge, their blue lights casting ominous blinking shadows across the forest floor. A little deeper in the woods, powerful lamps, set up by the forensic team, cast a piercing white glare over the scenes of crime officers as they carefully excavated and examined the forest floor. Police officers circled the area, scanning for clues or merely making their way through the unlit portions of the woods, directing their flashlight beams erratically like they were roving spotlights.

There would be gossip in the morning for sure, thought DI Nicholls, as he marched back toward the woods from Shona Alexander's house. He had really needed that cup of tea, but his lengthy conversation with Dougie and Shona had not revealed much. The boy had been more concerned with the mess he had made of his uniform, while his aunt seemed to live an incredibly isolated life at the big stone cottage, sentimentally named "Honeysuckle House." Despite living for fifteen years in Upton St. Mary, the closest she had come to giving him a lead was information concerning a land dispute that had been resolved eighteen months ago.

"Damnit!" Nicholls exclaimed into the dark night as he stubbed his boot on a large rock, almost stumbling head over heels. "Bloody rock!"

"You should have a torch," came a distant voice.

Nicholls looked up and was blinded by a powerful beam.

"Get that light out of my eyes!" he cried, angrily.

The beam was lowered, and as his eyes adjusted once again to the darkness, Nicholls saw the svelte figure of Harper Jones emerging from a cluster of trees.

"Sorry," DI Nicholls growled, as she drew closer, "I didn't realize it was you, Harper."

Not many people could elicit an apology from the Inspector, but Harper Jones demanded a certain respect, not least because she was one of the most brilliant pathologists in Britain and thus the Inspector's best hope for making some sense of the dead body in the woods.

Harper reached the Inspector and dropped her flashlight to her side. Even in the dim light, the Inspector could make out Harper's attractive face and upright bearing from the slivers of fading light that outlined her sharp features.

"This body's been here a while," Harper announced rather obviously, never one for small talk.

"How long?" the Inspector asked.

"We'll definitely need some time to figure it out. We're

still excavating it as carefully as possible, but my guess is that it's been buried there for well over a decade," she said.

"A decade?!"

Harper nodded, the moonlight skipping along her wavy hair. "Judging by the tissue quantities and the large number of roots that have grown around it. It's why the excavation still has some way to go."

Nicholls scratched his stubble and looked off toward the rhythmic blue glow being cast over the road.

"Is there anything else you can tell me?"

"Not much," Harper replied. "The body is in a fetal position, but that could mean anything. Defending against an attacker, huddling for warmth, disposal into a small hole – I don't know. That's your job."

Nicholls sighed deeply.

"We're never going to close a case this cold."

"There is one request I'd like to make," Harper said, maintaining her cool, assertive tone of voice despite her slight alarm at the Inspector's level of pessimism so early in the case.

"What's that?"

"I'd like a second opinion on this body. There's a lot of damage. It's difficult to ascertain what may be suspicious and what is the effect of decay, root growth, or simply the person's health in life. If I'm to make any judgments, I'd like the opinion of a forensic anthropologist."

"Do you have anybody in mind?"

For the first time, DI Nicholls detected a slightly regretful expression on the face of Harper Jones. He immediately dismissed it as a trick of the light, but Harper's somewhat wistful tone caused him to reconsider.

"Yes, actually."

"Okay. Well, bring them on board. I'm willing to pull in anyone who can help."

"That's good," Harper said, turning her head toward the road, "because I believe you're about to gain another ally."

Nicholls turned his head just in time to see a royal blue Mini Cooper pull up neatly behind a police car.

They watched as the large, unmistakable frame of Reverend Annabelle Dixon stepped out of the car and strode over to a nearby officer. After exchanging a few words, the constable gazed across the open stretch of land and pointed them out.

"Oh great," muttered Nicholls as Annabelle waved cheerily and began striding toward them, her smile visible even in the darkness. Harper raised her torch to reveal where they were, causing Annabelle to squint and stumble backwards in its blinding glare.

"Don't be proud," Harper said quietly, as she turned back toward the woods. "The Reverend is a smart cookie – and you're going to need all the help you can get with this one."

DI Nicholls gazed at the looming figure of Annabelle coming toward him, arms in full marching mode. When she got close, she took one step too many and clattered into him.

"Oops!" she said, unconvincingly. "Terribly dark, isn't it?"

"I'm afraid I'm busy, Reverend."

"Whatever's going on, Inspector?"

"I can't tell you. It's police business and classified. The one thing I can tell you is that you'll have to move along."

Disregarding the Inspector's dismissive tone, Annabelle decided to keep probing.

"It looks serious," she remarked, turning her head

toward the bright lamps of the forensic team. "I hope nobody was hurt."

Nicholls remained silent.

Annabelle was rather fond of the Inspector, more than a little fond if the rumors were to be believed, but she found his silence somewhat rude and unfriendly. Not least because she had only recently helped the Inspector solve a particularly tricky case. Nonetheless, Annabelle, her big, warm heart nearly always bursting with generosity, was determined, happy even, to place the blame for the Inspector's grumpiness on his long drive from Truro.

"Do you know whose body it is?" asked Annabelle, matter-of-factly.

The lines of DI Nicholls' frown were so deep that they were visible even by the faint light of the moon.

"Who told you there's a body?!"

"Nobody!" Annabelle responded jovially. "I simply noticed the forensic team working busily away. There are only two things I can think of that would demand so many people be plugging away at the ground – the discovery of treasure or a dead body. And you don't need so many policemen to unearth treasure!"

Annabelle laughed easily, unable to notice the Inspector's scowl in the darkness.

"I'll hope you're not planning to go around telling people there's a dead body in the woods, Reverend."

"Heavens, no! But I don't imagine it'll be a secret for long."

"Why's that?"

"Well, this road gets rather busy in the morning. It's one of the main commuter routes. You'll have plenty of rubber-neckers spreading gossip before most people have had their morning coffee!"

Nicholls sighed defeatedly. He hated gossip, especially when it involved a case of his and even more so when it involved a case as open as this. Once it started, he would be stumbling upon more red herrings than one would find in a mystery novel.

"Goodbye, Reverend," DI Nicholls said, decisively.

"Bye, Inspector!"

Both of them took a step in opposite directions before DI Nicholls looked back.

"Reverend? Your car is that way."

"Oh I know, Inspector. I'm still on my daily rounds and thought I'd pay the good Ms. Alexander a visit."

Nicholls considered trying to dissuade the Reverend, but he knew her well enough to know it was a lost cause. He nodded grimly and headed back toward the forensic team.

Annabelle was not immune to the Inspector's bizarrely downbeat manner, and she could only surmise that whatever – or whoever – was buried in the woods behind Honeysuckle House was a cause for great concern. If anyone knew what was happening, it would be Shona Alexander, her bouncy young nephew being the only one who frequented those woods daily.

She walked briskly closer to the welcoming light of Honeysuckle House's decorated windows. Pots of herbs and aromatic flowers were neatly arranged beneath them. As she opened the wooden gate to Shona's wildflower garden, she noticed Constable Raven coming in the opposite direction.

"Constable Raven!"

"Oh, hello Reverend. Strange to see you out this late."

"It's not that late, Constable. The days are simply getting shorter."

Jim Raven looked up at the sky.

"I suppose you're right. It's going to get cold soon, I'd better get my boiler fixed."

"Constable," Annabelle said, seriously. "What is all this fuss about in the woods?"

Constable Raven shook his head slowly. "I'm sorry, Reverend. I'm under strict orders from Detective Inspector Nicholls to keep this as secret as possible."

"I had a feeling you might say that. But it must be something rather concerning to have the Inspector so worked up."

Raven allowed himself a wry smile. "Are you referring by chance to the chief's foul mood? I'm afraid that's got nothing to do with the case. He's been acting like he swallowed a wasp for weeks now."

"Why?" asked Annabelle, leaning forward with keen interest.

Raven shook his head.

"Constable Colback tells me nobody in Truro has the faintest idea what's bothering him. It's an even bigger mystery than the body in the woods. Ah—"

Raven stuttered, looking for something to say that would distract Annabelle from his slip of the tongue. Annabelle chuckled.

"Relax, Constable. I had already figured that out."

Raven's shoulders dropped a full inch, deflated. "It's nice of you to fib, Reverend, but I shouldn't have said that."

"Forget about it, Constable," Annabelle said, stepping past him. "I'll see you about the village, I expect."

"Yeah," muttered Constable Raven, still shaking his head at his own stupidity.

"You're not planning to ask Ms. Alexander about this, are you?"

Annabelle smiled. "I was actually planning to ask her how she was managing to keep her basil so vital at this time of year, but I expect this will be a rather unavoidable subject."

Constable Raven nodded as if receiving bad news, before turning around and making his way out of the garden and back toward the crime scene. As he went on his way, he decided that his spilling the beans was no fault of his own. It was Reverend Annabelle. She simply had a very sharp knack for uncovering secrets.

To get your copy of Body in the Woods, visit the link below:
https://www.alisongolden.com/body-in-the-woods

REVERENTIAL RECIPES

CONTINUE ON TO
CHECK OUT THE
RECIPES FOR
GOODIES
FEATURED IN
THIS BOOK...

WICKED WALNUT CUPCAKES
WITH MAGNIFICENT MAPLE BUTTERCREAM FROSTING

For the cupcakes:
¾ cup (1 ½ sticks) unsalted butter
1 cup soft brown sugar, packed
1 cup sugar
3 eggs
3 cups flour
1 ½ teaspoon baking powder
¼ teaspoon salt
1 ¼ cup whole milk
1 teaspoon vanilla extract
Walnut butter (see recipe)

For the frosting:
¾ cup (1 ½ sticks) unsalted butter
2 cups powdered sugar
Walnut butter (see recipe)
½ teaspoon molasses
½ teaspoon maple extract
1 teaspoon vanilla extract
2-3 tablespoons water

½ teaspoon walnuts, finely chopped

For the walnut butter:
1 cup shelled walnuts
2 tablespoons butter
3 tablespoons water (as needed)
Dash salt

Preheat the oven to 350°F/180°C. Line cupcake tins with paper liners. To make the walnut butter, mix all ingredients in food processor until well blended. Add water to make the consistency creamy, like mildly chunky peanut butter.

To make cupcakes, cream butter and sugars until light and fluffy. Beat in eggs one at a time. Add sifted dry ingredients, and slowly blend in milk. Stir in vanilla extract and fold in six tablespoons of the walnut butter. Reserve remainder of butter for frosting. Spoon cupcake batter into paper liners, filling them about three quarters full.

Bake the cupcakes until a toothpick inserted into the center comes out clean, about 20 to 25 minutes. Leave to cool completely.

For the frosting, cream together unsalted butter and sugar. Gradually add remainder of walnut butter, molasses, maple extract, and vanilla extract. Add water, one tablespoon at a time, until mixture is fluffy and creamy. Top cupcakes with frosting, and add finely chopped walnuts for decoration.

Makes approximately 30 cupcakes.

BEATIFIC BAKLAVA

1⅔ cups sugar
1½ cups water
2 teaspoons rose water
2 teaspoons orange blossom water
⅔ cup honey
2 cinnamon sticks
2 (5-inch x ½-inch) strips orange peel
2 cup (2 sticks) butter, melted
1 cup chopped walnuts
½ cup chopped pecans
½ cup chopped almonds
1 teaspoon ground cinnamon
½ teaspoon ground allspice
15 phyllo pastry sheets frozen, thawed

Stir 1⅓ cups sugar, water, rose water, orange blossom water, honey, cinnamon sticks, and orange peel in saucepan over medium heat until sugar dissolves. Increase heat and bring to boil, stirring continuously for 10-15 minutes or until consistency is thick like syrup. Remove from heat, and chill until cold.

Preheat oven to 325°F/160°C. Line a 13 x 9 x 2-inch metal baking pan with parchment paper, and brush with a little of the melted butter. Mix walnuts, pecans, almonds, cinnamon, allspice, and the remaining ⅓ cup sugar in a medium bowl.

Fold one sheet of phyllo pastry in half to form a 12 x 9-inch rectangle. Place folded sheet in prepared pan. Brush with melted butter. Repeat with four more folded sheets, brushing top of each with butter.

Sprinkle half of nut mixture over the top of the pastry. Repeat with five more folded sheets, brushing the top of each with butter. Sprinkle remaining nut mixture over the top. Add five more folded sheets of pastry, again brushing the top of each with melted butter.

Using a sharp knife, make seven diagonal cuts across the phyllo pastry, cutting through top layers only and spacing cuts evenly. Repeat in opposite direction, with cuts crossing in the middle to form a diamond pattern. Bake in the oven until golden brown, around 30 to 40 minutes.

Strain white foam, cinnamon sticks, and orange peels from syrup. Spoon 1¼ cups syrup over hot baklava. Cover and refrigerate or dispose of remaining syrup.

Cut baklava along lines all the way through layers. Cover and let stand at room temperature for four hours before eating. Can be made one day ahead. Do not wrap, or it will become soggy. Best if served individually. Can be chilled.

Makes approximately 30 pieces.

CHASTE CHIA SEED AND COCONUT MACAROONS

1 egg, beaten
¼ cup sugar
¾ cup shredded coconut
1 tablespoon chia seeds

Preheat oven to 350°F/180°C. Put the egg in a mixing bowl. Beat the sugar into the eggs with a fork, then stir in the coconut and chia seeds. Press the mixture, a few spoonfuls at a time, into a small eggcup, then turn upside down and tap out onto a baking sheet to form small rounds.

Bake for about 20 minutes or until golden-brown. Remove from the oven and leave to cool for a few minutes before transferring to a wire rack to cool completely.

Makes 7-8.

ANGELIC ALMOND CUPCAKES
WITH ABUNDANT ALMOND BUTTER FROSTING

For the cupcakes:
1 ½ cups flour
1 ¾ teaspoons baking powder
1 cup white sugar
½ cup (1 stick) unsalted butter, softened
2 eggs
1 teaspoon vanilla extract
2 tablespoons almond butter
1 cup vanilla flavored almond milk
1 pinch salt

For the frosting:
½ cup (1 stick) unsalted butter, softened
1 ½ cups powdered sugar
2 tablespoons almond butter
½ teaspoon vanilla extract
2 tablespoons water (or as needed for consistency)
¼ cup almond slivers

Preheat the oven to 350°F/180°C. Line cupcake tins with paper liners. In a bowl, sift together the flour and baking powder.

In a separate bowl, using an electric mixer, cream together the sugar and butter until well blended. Beat in the eggs, one at a time, and stir in the vanilla. Gradually beat in the flour mixture, slowly adding in the almond milk, almond butter, and salt. Make sure all the ingredients are well blended. Spoon mixture into each paper liner, filling them about ¾ full.

Bake the cupcakes until a toothpick inserted into the center comes out clean, about 20 to 25 minutes. Leave to cool completely.

To make frosting, sift powdered sugar and beat together with butter. Add almond butter to sugar and butter mixture. Add vanilla extract. Add water, one tablespoon at a time, until mixture is fluffy and creamy. Top cupcakes with frosting and add almond slivers for decoration.

Makes approximately 16 cupcakes.

All ingredients are available from your local store or online retailer.

You can find printable versions of these recipes and links to the ingredients used in them at https://www.alisongolden. com/murder-at-the-mansion-recipes/

For a limited time, you can get the first books in each of my series - *Chaos in Cambridge, The Case of the Screaming Beauty, Hunted, and Mardi Gras Madness* - plus updates about new releases, promotions, and other Insider exclusives, by signing up for my mailing list at:

https://www.alisongolden.com/annabelle

BOOKS BY ALISON GOLDEN

FEATURING INSPECTOR DAVID GRAHAM

The Case of the Screaming Beauty

The Case of the Hidden Flame

The Case of the Fallen Hero

The Case of the Broken Doll

The Case of the Missing Letter

The Case of the Pretty Lady

The Case of the Forsaken Child

FEATURING ROXY REINHARDT

Mardi Gras Madness

New Orleans Nightmare

Louisiana Lies

As A. J. Golden

FEATURING DIANA HUNTER

Hunted (Prequel)

Snatched

Stolen

Chopped

Exposed

ABOUT THE AUTHOR

Alison Golden is the *USA Today* bestselling author of the Inspector David Graham mysteries, a traditional British detective series, and two cozy mystery series featuring main characters Reverend Annabelle Dixon and Roxy Reinhardt. As A. J. Golden, she writes the Diana Hunter thriller series.

Alison was raised in Bedfordshire, England. Her aim is to write stories that are designed to entertain, amuse, and calm. Her approach is to combine creative ideas with excellent writing and edit, edit, edit. Alison's mission is simple: To write excellent books that have readers clamoring for more.

Alison is based in the San Francisco Bay Area with her husband and twin sons. She splits her time between London and San Francisco.

For up-to-date promotions and release dates of upcoming books, sign up for the latest news here: https://www.alisongolden.com/annabelle.

For more information:
www.alisongolden.com
alison@alisongolden.com

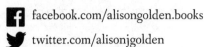

facebook.com/alisongolden.books

twitter.com/alisonjgolden

instagram.com/alisonjgolden

THANK YOU

Thank you for taking the time to read *Murder in the Mansion*. If you enjoyed it, please consider telling your friends or posting a short review. Word of mouth is an author's best friend and very much appreciated.
Thank you,